A Secret Staircase

A Murder at the Morrisey
Book Two

Eryn Scott

KRISTOPHERSON
PRESS
Publishing

Copyright © 2023 by Eryn Scott

Published by Kristopherson Press

All rights reserved.

www.erynscott.com

erynwrites@gmail.com

Facebook: @erynscottauthor

Sign up for my newsletter to hear about new releases and sales!

No part of this book may be reproduced in any form or by any electronic or mechanical means, including information storage and retrieval systems, without written permission from the author, except for the use of brief quotations in a book review.

Cover design by Chris M - Torn Edge Design

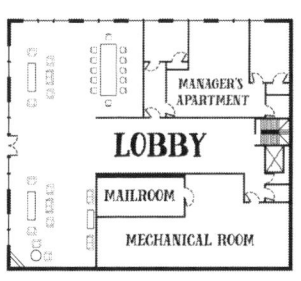

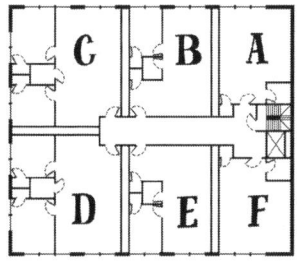
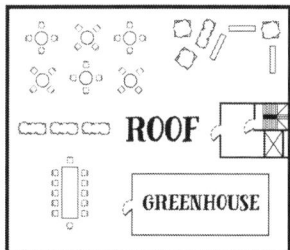

LIST OF APARTMENTS AND RESIDENTS

	ROOF	
5C - ALYSSA VERLICE		5F - BAILEY LUNA
5B - IRIS FINLEY		5E - FOR RENT
5A - MEG DAWSON		5D - EDNA FELDNER
4C - W. UNDERWOOD		4F - PAUL KELLY
4B - LAURENCE TURNER		4E - WINNIE WISTERIA
4A - RONNY ARBURY		4D - GREG, OLLIE, LEIA PORTER
3C - KATE, OWEN, FINN, BRYCE O'BRIEN		3F - FATIMA AND URBANE JUNT
		3E - ANDREW SASIN
3B - OPAL HALIFAX		3D - SHIRLEY AND BETHANY ROSENBLOOM
3A - JULIAN CREED		
2C - DANICA AND DUSTIN MCNAIRY		2F - HAYDEN AND TEAL NUTTERS
		2E - ARTURO CORTEZ
2B - DARIUS ROWLAND		2D - VALARIE, VICTORIA, NOEL, MIA YOUNG
2A - CASCADE GRYFFON		
	LOBBY	
	BUILDING MANAGER - NANCY LEWANDOWSKI	

One

Pity was not an emotion I was used to experiencing when it came to the stalwart manager of the Morrisey apartment building.

Nancy Lewandowski was the definition of confidence and capability. She could settle a debate with a well-timed lift of a single eyebrow, and I'd seen grown men skitter away from her in fear whenever she used her *no-nonsense* voice.

But as she stood there, fingers gripping her podium, sympathy overwhelmed me. Even her reading glasses, which always seemed to balance perfectly on the tip of her nose, sat askew as she tried to regain control of the meeting.

"Everyone needs to calm down," Nancy called, her voice trembling.

I squirmed in my seat, my sweaty legs sticking to the chair as my neighbors continued to lob complaints at her.

Normally, Nancy seemed to look forward to building meetings as if they were her own personal Christmas each month. Gathering everyone to chat about building matters while she stood behind her podium, checking items off her agenda, was her happy place.

This particular meeting was different. The residents were hot, scared, and tired. Hot because the July sun was streaming unrelentingly through the tall lobby windows. Scared because I'd recently uncovered secret passages hidden within the walls of our Seattle building. Not just any passages, either, but ones specifically created with the intention of sneaking into our apartments unseen. And tired because the meeting was dragging into its second sweaty hour, and the chairs, which we usually only had to endure for thirty minutes or so, began to feel like torture devices.

"I haven't slept a wink since Meg found those passages." Winnie Wisteria dramatically placed the back of her hand to her forehead like a silver-screen damsel.

I turned to my right, where my best friend, Ripley, usually sat. Even though she was a ghost, and I couldn't talk to her around living people, her commentary and the faces we would make at each other made building meetings bearable. But instead of Ripley, Julian from the third floor sat there today.

Ever since the ghostly guy Ripley had fallen for had moved on last week, she'd barely left the apartment. Clark's disappearance had affected her more than I'd ever experienced. And seeing how I was the reason she was stuck on this plane of existence, unable to move on like other ghosts, I wasn't sure how to help her get out of this kind of depression.

Unaware of my inner struggle, and taking my turning toward him as commentary on Winnie's dramatic statement,

Julian said, "If she hadn't slept in days, she would've gone mad by now." Then he tilted his head to the side as if, on second thought, that might explain a lot about Winnie.

Nancy looked from Winnie to the rest of the residents. "I know. I'm sorry it's taken me so long to call this meeting. I've been dealing with the police and then lawyers..."

The first item on Nancy's agenda that day had been to let us know that apartment 5E would be rented out to help Quentin pay for the myriad of fees he would incur as he went to trial.

"The point is," Nancy continued, her tone sharpening as if she'd suddenly remembered who she was, that she could handle this, "we're here to discuss what to do next."

Winnie let out a dramatic sigh that included a fair bit of whimpering.

Paul, Winnie's neighbor on the fourth floor, put a hand on her shoulder. "It's okay, Winnie. Quentin's gone. We're safe now."

Julian shot out of his seat next to me, making me jump in surprise. "Safe? We might be safe from murderers, but *anyone* can get into our apartments. They could steal our stuff."

"Who are you worried about?" Alyssa asked, turning in her seat to face Julian. "Because, right now, the only people with access to the passages are those of us in the building." My fifth-floor neighbor cut her eyes across to the man next to me, staring daggers.

Wendell Underwood cleared his throat and flicked two fingers into the air. "I'd like for it to be listed that I think the secret passages are awesome."

The lobby went silent as everyone turned to the fourth-floor resident ... the one with far too many snakes for any one person. A collective shiver slithered through the lobby.

"There's no *list*, Wendell," Nancy said through a tired exhale. Her attention swept over us. "I called this meeting, hoping we could all get on the same page about what to do about these passages. But based on the differing opinions I've had *yelled* at me over the last hour"—Nancy glowered disappointedly at the naysayers—"I'd say we're not going to agree."

A few residents opened their mouths and scowled as if they were going to protest, but Nancy flicked an index finger in the air as she continued.

"The fact is, you each own your apartment, and I cannot legally tell you what to do with your property." She cut a glare at Wendell, who cowered under her scrutiny.

"So, people will be allowed to keep their passages open?" Danica McNairy shot to her feet, holding her pregnant belly.

Nancy patted the air. "Yes, but if your passage is locked from the inside, it shouldn't matter to you." She held Danica's gaze until the woman reclaimed her seat.

"And I'm guessing this'll come out of our own pockets?" Arturo scoffed. As one of our buildings' self-proclaimed Conversationalists, Art constantly talked about how he was on a fixed income.

Nancy's chin jutted forward. "Of course it will. Just like it would be if you decided you wanted to buy a new fridge or install a new door buzzer. And until I can find a new handyman, we'll be on our own to deal with repairs." At that statement, Nancy's shoulders sank forward.

Whispers trailed around the room. No one wanted to talk about—or even think about—Quentin. It was too soon.

Nancy kneaded her fingers into her temple. "I *will* give everyone a few months off from paying building dues to ease the financial burden." For once, positive sounds spilled from the crowd at that statement. Nancy looked down at the podium as she continued thinking and tapped her pen like a conductor with a baton. "Okay. How about this? Creepy as it was, Wendell's comment about a list was actually kind of inspired."

Wendell ducked his head and waved to the group as if he wasn't completely sure it was a compliment, but he would take what he could get.

Nancy's nostrils flared as she inhaled. "I'm going to start a list of who would like their passageway covered, and I will see if I can get a quote from a contractor. That way I'm doing most of the legwork for you. You just have to pay them. How does that sound? Better, huh?" Nancy pointed her pen at various residents, daring them to tell her it wasn't helpful.

"That *would* help. Thank you, Nance," Julian said.

Others followed his statement with their own cowed thank-yous directed at our building manager.

"I'm just going to start from floor two and move up." Nancy held her pen at the ready as she called out to Cascade, who lived in apartment 2A.

By the time she'd gone through floors two and three, the ratio was sitting at about two to one in favor of having the passages closed off. The other side either didn't care that they were there, said they would fix it themselves, or they just didn't have the funds to do it at the moment and would get around to it later.

After recording Ronnie Arbury's choice for apartment 4A, Nancy's lips twisted into a question. "Hmmm. What should we do about Laurence?" Every eye turned to me in the seconds that followed. "Meg, do you want to ask him?"

My heartbeat spiked at Nancy's request. *Why? Because I'm in love with him and everyone knows?* My worried thoughts bounced around inside my mind.

Sucking air in through my nose, I let the oxygen flow through me, calming my anxiety. In that much more rational state, I reasoned that the request wasn't about my crush on Laurie. We were friends. The whole building knew that. That was why they'd asked me.

Nodding, I held up my phone and wiggled it in the air, accepting the job nonverbally since I didn't trust my voice. I did a quick calculation to see what time it was in Japan.

It was something I'd been doing a lot over the past four days, ever since Laurie left for the island in the Pacific Ocean, almost five thousand miles away from me. Unlike every other time I'd added the sixteen hours to figure out the difference, I got a number that wasn't in the middle of the night or too early.

Eight o'clock in the morning wasn't an unreasonable time to text him. So, I typed out the message.

> Hey! I hope you're settling in okay over there. We're having a Morrisey meeting, and Nance wants to know what you want to do about your passageway entrance. Most people are having a contractor secure theirs shut from the inside. A few are leaving theirs alone.

Knowing at least half of the residents would still be watching me even though Nancy had moved on to the other fourth-floor apartments, I schooled my expression so I wouldn't look too eager as I waited for Laurie's response. But nothing could've helped me hold back my excitement as three dots appeared at the bottom of the screen, showing me Laurie was responding.

> Oh man, I miss it there so much. Japan is beautiful, but I've been working a ton since the second I landed. Um, yes to the closing of the passage. What are you going to do with yours?

Rolling my lips to hide my giddy smile, I glanced up and made eye contact with Nancy, waiting until she was done documenting Paul Kelly's choice for apartment 4F.

"Laurie's a yes and so am I," I told her, knowing I'd be the next person she'd call since I lived in 5A.

Nancy wrote down our decisions with a satisfied nod. "You tell him hi for us," she said. It wasn't a question.

I gave her a thumbs-up, showing I would. My response recorded, I turned my attention back to replying to Laurie.

> You kidding? I'm closing that thing off for good. I spent more time in those passages than I ever want to again. *shudder* Also, everyone says hello and that they can't possibly live without you.

> I don't blame you for feeling that way. I also don't blame them for missing me.

After that came a winking emoji. Grinning like a fool, I responded.

> I can see that Japan has humbled you. Where's the self-assured Laurie I know and love?

I worried my lip for a moment before sending the word *love*, knowing it was all too close to the truth. But if the past week had taught me anything, it was that I could be brave.

> Oh, he's here, hoping for a play-by-play of that meeting. Meg, you cannot leave me hanging.

I suppressed a giggle, more than willing to fill him in on the antics of our neighbors. Tilting the phone to my left, where there was an empty seat, and no one would be able to read my screen, I typed out a response.

> Well, Julian's convinced everyone's going to use the passages to sneak in and steal his "stuff," which makes me SO interested to see what kind of stuff he has that he thinks we would want.

> Haha. That's so Julian. My guess: it's not anything cool. It's gotta be something weird and embarrassing, and he doesn't want us to see it.

> Ah, like a collection of dolls.

> Lol. Stuffed animals, maybe?

Picking up my head for a moment so I could relay what else was going on in the meeting, I typed out what I saw.

> Now Winnie is complaining that there's no way she can possibly wait for the contractor to close off her passage. She says she hasn't slept since I found them, which Julian said has to be a lie.

> I don't think anything Winnie says is true.

I had to agree with the man. When Winnie wasn't being incredibly secretive, she gave vague, cagey answers that made us all sure the woman was hiding something.

About to write out a response, I stopped when I saw the three dots appear again. Laurie was writing more.

> The last few days have felt like an eternity. I'm missing Leo a ton, but do you know who I'm also missing?

I held my breath. Of course, he would miss his dog. I stared at the screen, waiting for him to answer the rhetorical question.

> You.

"Me!" In my surprise, I gasped the word out loud.

"Oh, good. Thank you, Meg," Nancy said. "That's very sweet of you. Just come see me once we're all done here."

My gaze snapped up from my phone to Nancy's podium. *Wait. Had I just accidentally volunteered for something?* From the relief written on my fellow residents' faces, it was something they were glad to get out of.

> I miss you too. But, oh gosh. I wasn't paying attention, and I think I just volunteered for something. Stay tuned.

> Edge of my seat here, Dawson.

I tucked my phone in my pocket and picked my way to the podium as people began to fold and stack the meeting chairs. I stopped in front of Nancy. My body tensed as I waited to hear what I'd volunteered to do.

She clapped her hands together. "The piece of wood I'm talking about is in the back right corner in the mechanical room. There are a bunch stacked there, so just pick the one that has the fewest spiders and bring it up to Winnie's floor. We'll just wedge it in her closet until I can find a contractor." Nancy held her big jangly ring of keys out toward me, specifically finding the one that would let me into the dusty, expansive room that housed our furnace, generator, hot water heater, and pretty much everything else that ran the building.

Blinking, I pushed past her comment about spiders and

started toward the mechanical room. Keeping the key I needed pinched between two fingers, I fished my phone out of my pocket and hit the dictate button since I only had one hand free now.

> And the answer is ... Winnie refuses to wait, so I have to go find a piece of spider-infested wood to bring up and block her passage now.

> I mean, Meg, she hasn't slept in days. She needs this.

He followed up his text with a laughing emoji, just in case I hadn't picked up on his sarcasm.

> Naturally.

> Well, good luck. Let me know how it goes.

> I will.

Sad as I was about ending our conversation, I needed to concentrate on what I was doing. Laurie's earlier comment about the last few days feeling like an eternity stuck with me. They really had, for more than one reason. Laurie wasn't the only one who was working nonstop. I'd spent hours—an increasing number each day—working to undo the self-doubt and negative talk that had caused me to quit art in New York earlier that year. I'd painted something new every day since, and I felt my joy returning.

Actually, I'd been painting when my neighbors interrupted to tell me about the building meeting. Which meant the quicker I got this errand done for Nancy, the sooner I could get back to my artwork.

The hot, musty smell of the mechanical room hit me in the face as I entered. I skirted past the mailroom and headed for the back right corner. Ducking around pipes and taking care not to step in the few puddles of water accumulating from who-knows-which leaking part, I almost didn't see the boards at first. They were gray with age instead of the orangey-tan of newly cut wood, and they blended in with the concrete walls.

Nancy was right; there were quite a few pieces of wood of different sizes. I slid the first one away from the group, propping it against the water heater tank. It was too small, though it definitely seemed spider-free, which I wasn't sure was going to be a guarantee as I dug deeper into the stack.

The next few were still too small. The edges bit into my fingers as I dragged each piece away and put it to the side so I could access the next one. I threw my hair up into a bun to get it out of the way as sweat formed on my neck from all the work. The penultimate board looked to be the right size, but it also had the biggest spider I'd ever seen clutching to the side, and I didn't want to take a chance. I pushed that forward, so I could slide the last board out from against the wall.

But as I moved the final piece of wood, a gust of air whooshed past me. It smelled even mustier than the rest of the place, if that was possible. Pulling it out all the way, I uncovered a threshold. The opening was just a touch smaller than a standard doorway, and it was edged with brick, inlaid within the concrete wall.

Another room? That didn't seem possible. I was standing up against the side of the building. But as I examined the southernmost wall, I noticed this section popped in about four feet more than the rest. I'd never thought about the discrepancy, or what might be housed there, since all the exterior walls of our building were straight.

I stepped through and used my phone's flashlight to investigate. A pitch-black staircase opened before me, my light only reaching about halfway down.

"Another secret passageway?" I asked to no one with a groan.

That was the last thing we needed. We were still dealing with the fallout from the last secret I discovered in this building. I could just picture the pandemonium now. This would surely break Winnie.

I *almost* turned around, but my curiosity got the better of me. Maybe I could just check it out, make sure there was nothing I needed to tell Nancy about, and then put the boards back so no one knew about it.

Resolved, I stepped down onto the staircase, recognizing that my light shook along with my fingers as they gripped my phone.

Two

As I descended into the unknown, I expected the temperature to drop, something that would've been welcome on such a hot summer day. But the air merely got hotter and stuffier as I took step after step. As the humidity rose, the furrows in my forehead deepened, and I waited for the old, sloping staircase to spit me out into the creepy basement of our building.

Like most buildings in Pioneer Square, the Morrisey's "first" level was actually underground. I remembered back to the explanation I'd heard when Penny and I had taken a tour of the Underground when I was a kid.

Because they'd built Seattle on a tide flat, the toilets during the first iteration of the city would back up each time the tide came in. After the Great Fire of 1889 decimated the primarily wooden-built downtown, the city took the opportunity to rebuild. They made sure everything was made of stone, brick, or steel, and they raised the streets, placing the sewer line inside the raised portion of each roadway so it would be above sea level, effectively fixing the backup problem. That restructure lead to what Seattleites refer to as the Underground.

In the early nineteen hundreds, the city condemned the Underground after the rat infestation became so bad that they feared it would lead to an outbreak of the bubonic plague. After that, the underground level became a hotbed for crime and illegal activity in the city, housing many hidden drinking establishments during Prohibition.

Over the decades, the Underground was closed off, sealed up in an effort to quell the illegal activities encouraged by the hidden aspect of it all. Some building owners boarded off the area and had never reopened it. Others rented out the space to the various walking tours that operated in the square. And some cleaned up the area, making it useable once more as either an extension of the building's square footage or for storage.

Whatever it had been before, the Morrisey's basement had been allocated as resident storage sometime in the seventies. While the basement had been cleared of the rusted, broken, or dusty remnants of the early nineteen hundreds, we'd just gone and replaced it with our own from this century. Nancy stored larger pieces of furniture down there, or old broken pieces she was going to "get someone to fix someday." To be fair to Nance, it was a time-honored tradition started by building managers before her—like her predecessor, Opal Halifax.

That wasn't the only thing down there either. A small cadre of ghosts dwelled in the basement. Having been able to see and speak to spirits since I was born, I wasn't easily scared by the souls who had yet to pass on. Heck, my very best friend in the whole world, Ripley, was a ghost. But the basement ghosts were different.

After a terrifying run-in with them as a child, I'd refused to go back into the basement. This would be my first time returning after all these years.

As I reached the bottom of this staircase, however, it didn't turn left into the half-remembered Morrisey basement full of old furniture and my childhood fears. The staircase jutted to the right, spilling me into the wild, untended, and incredibly dark Seattle Underground.

Standing in what used to be an alley between the buildings, I stepped forward. Shining my flashlight into the inky darkness, I found a mostly open area, proving that the building to the right of the Morrisey had opted for the first option; they'd completely closed off access to their first floor and hadn't bothered to maintain it. Piles of rubble sat next to rusted pipes. The floors sloped down and jutted up, littered with debris.

The old windows and doorways of the building's first floor were either encrusted with dirt or broken instead of being filled with concrete to create a solid wall like the Morrisey's. Half a sink leaned against stacks of unused timber and support beams. Water dripped from the ceiling to my right, even though it hadn't rained in weeks.

As my flashlight swept slowly over the place, my heart was in my throat. Any second, I expected one of the nasty basement ghosts to jump out and scare me, just like when I was a kid.

But it seemed to be just me. And the rats. My light

reflected off their beady eyes, and their small screeches echoed through the space as I wandered forward into the underground alleyway between the buildings. To my left was a brick wall where the office building behind the Morrisey had been closed off, probably for storage like ours.

Something skittered right behind me, and I rushed forward to get away from it. In my haste, my toe caught on the uneven floor and I pitched forward, my glorious fall illuminated by the flashlight on my phone. Really not wanting to be without the phone—and the flashlight attached to it—I clung desperately to the thing as I landed on my knees and elbows with an *oomph* and a cloud of dust.

Checking behind me to make sure there wasn't a rat still in hot pursuit of my flesh, I dusted off my arms. There was a piece of wood to my right, and I used it to pull myself up.

But that turned out to be a bad idea. The rotted wood gave way, cracking as it snapped in half, sending me back down to the ground. This time, I was on my butt. I was really getting tired of it down here.

As the dust cleared, however, I realized the piece of wood had been hiding something: an alcove akin to a closet sat behind where the wood had been. Inside it, under layers of dust, were the bones of a full skeleton.

I let out a strangled cry and crawled back. "Gross, gross, gross," I whispered. My voice shook as I got as far away from the skeleton as I could.

"Rude. I'm not gross." The voice came from behind me.

Shaking with fear, I studied the skeleton. It hadn't moved at all, even though the voice seemed to take ownership of the bones. I slowly turned around, shining my flashlight in the direction of the voice.

"You?" I asked when I found a young woman standing just behind me, staring down at where I'd fallen.

She looked just about as solid as my arm, but the light of my flashlight bounced through her body, refracting slightly through her shape.

A ghost. The spirit attached to the skeleton I'd stumbled upon, I realized, glancing over my shoulder.

She was dressed in a sparkly nineteen twenties' flapper dress, the sad remnants of which still clung to the dusty bones behind me. Her brown hair was styled in pin curls that had been shellacked to her scalp and then pulled into a low bun at the nape of her neck. Based on her outfit, I was semi-surprised that she didn't appear in black-and-white or the sepia tone of old photographs. Ironically, she also wore the wide-eyed expression of someone who'd seen a ghost.

"You can see me?" she whispered. Her eyes doubled in size as she took in my phone and the flashlight. "That's the strangest flashlight I've ever seen." She sucked in a breath. "Are you from the future?" The way she studied me made me very aware of my messy hair and dusty clothes.

Focusing on her question, I tilted the phone left and right. "Uh, yeah. And, yes, I can see you. Both of you." I followed the statement with a cringe as I glanced from her spirit to her skeleton.

Despite my morbid comment, the ghost bounced on the balls of her feet. "This is amazing," she squealed. "I've been stuck down here *forever*." Covering her mouth with her ghostly hands, she said, "You can help me take my body out of this old closet so I can leave. Finally."

There was *no* way I was touching that skeleton. Luckily, I wouldn't have to. "Um ... that's not how it works," I told her, getting to my feet and brushing the dust off my shorts.

Her expression fell. "You mean I'm *actually* going to be stuck down here forever?"

"No, I mean, you can leave right now. You're not tied to where your body is." At least, I didn't think she would be. Other than Ripley, most ghosts I'd met over the years followed the same rules. "You can only appear in places you visited when you were alive, though. If you try to go beyond those parameters, you'll vanish and reappear in the place you had the strongest connection to."

"That's what keeps happening every time I try to leave here." Her red lips twisted into a frown. "I can walk through walls down here, but the moment I try to go up there, I vanish and reappear here, next to me." She pouted.

I pulled in a breath through my nose and chewed on my lip as I thought. Ripley's existence showed me there were exceptions to the ghostly rules, so there was always a possibility that this ghost was right, that she was limited to staying with her bones.

"There's an easy way to check," I told her. "Picture a place you want to go and imagine yourself standing there." It was how Ripley described the way she hopped around from one location to another in the blink of an eye.

The ghost's eyes traveled up and down me, taking in my shorts and T-shirt. "What year is it?"

"Two thousand twenty-three," I answered.

She looked like she was straight out of the nineteen twenties, which meant...

"I've been down here for a hundred years?" She gasped, staggering backward. "Is anything even the same?"

A smile spread across my face. Part of what I loved about living in Pioneer Square was the rich history. It was Seattle's first neighborhood, and the city worked hard to preserve what they could.

"A lot more than you'd think," I said. Snapping my fingers, I added, "The pergola in Pioneer Square. Was that around when you were alive?"

The woman blinked. "It was. It went up when I was a little girl."

"It's still there. It's a small urban park now. Picture yourself standing underneath it," I instructed.

Her brows compressed in concentration. But nothing happened. Her thin shoulders dropped. "I can't do it. I'm stuck here forever." Tears crowded her big doe eyes, glimmering in the light of my flashlight.

"Don't give up just yet. There are a few other things we can try." I stepped forward. "What's your name?"

"Addison." She sniffed.

I placed a hand on my chest. "I'm Meg. It's nice to meet you, Addison."

"My best friends called me Addy."

Happiness sparked inside my chest. "Well, Addy, my best friend calls me Megs, and I think we should do a little more exploring. You were obviously here at some point during your life." I gestured to her body. "Let's figure out how you got down here."

As I turned around, I realized I'd lost track of the way I'd come. Where was the staircase to the Morrisey? I wasn't sure if my quaking fingers were a product of fear or holding my phone forward for so long as a flashlight.

Seeing a pathway to my right, I headed in that direction. "Follow me. If you disappear, call out, and I'll come back to you. We'll try a different route."

We tried three different pathways, two of which made Addy vanish. Each time, we had to go back to her skeleton to start over. The third one we tried, however, skirting along the raised city street, seemed to be the one.

Above us, light filtered through a grate filled with purple glass. I'd learned about these skylights on that Underground tour as well. They'd been installed to let light in, but the once-clear glass had turned purple over time—a reaction of manganese in the glass to sun exposure. Similar purple glass skylights were littered throughout the streets of Pioneer Square.

Addy and I paused to stare up at the muted purple light streaming down from above. Above us, people walked over the skylight, none the wiser about what lay beneath their feet. I wasn't even sure if they would hear me if I called for help. We continued on.

"This path is working," Addy whispered in a tone so high-pitched that it hurt my ears.

I nodded, but concentrated on the small area we were moving through. Between the uneven ground, the slowly sinking concrete, and the rusty pipes and beams sticking out haphazardly, it was no wonder I'd fallen earlier. Without Addy's constant chatter, the darkness and quiet closed in on me, making me feel like I was suffocating.

A sweet scent wafted toward me in the musty space. It smelled like peaches. Was I having a stroke or something?

"Do you smell that?" I asked Addy before remembering that ghosts couldn't smell.

Ripley and I had hypothesized about this over the years. Why could they see and hear, but not smell or taste? The only guess we had was that the reason spirits were stuck on this plane of existence was to take care of their unfinished business, so they were left with the senses they would need to do that, talking and listening. The others were unnecessary toward their ends.

Addy cocked an eyebrow at me.

"Never mind," I mumbled, turning the flashlight back in front of me. I inhaled sharply. "Stairs," I whispered. They looked old. Bingo.

Addy and I rushed up the single flight, stopping at a metal door, but it wouldn't budge.

"See if you can get through." I wafted my hands toward the door.

If she could climb the stairs, that meant she'd been this way before. Which also meant that even if it was locked for me, it shouldn't be for her.

Her eyes went wide, and she stepped through the door. A moment later, she returned. A huge grin sparkled on her face, almost as flashy as her dress.

"I'm free." She spun around, her outstretched arms slicing through me, creating odd shivers. Pulling them into her body, she said, "Ew. That felt weird. Sorry. Thank you so much, Meg! This is amazing. I can't wait to explore the city."

Unable to hold back a joyful chuckle at her excitement, I said, "Glad I could help."

But even though this staircase looked to be Addy's exit, it was not mine. Turning my attention back toward the Underground, I started back down the stairs. I needed to find the Morrisey staircase and get out of there.

I was halfway down the staircase when I realized Addy was following me.

I hesitated. "Um... You're free, Addy. You don't have to come with me. Go explore. See what's different, like you said you wanted to." I pulled my lips into an encouraging smile and gestured toward the locked door.

"I know..." Her toe drew a line that wouldn't show up on the dusty stairs. "The least I can do is help you back."

"Are you sure you'll be able to find your way?" I asked, worried the ghost would be stuck down here for another century if I left her in the dark again.

She nodded resolutely. "I know where I am now. My family owned a building on this block. See?" She disappeared and reappeared.

"That must be why your spirit is so strong here," I said, motioning to her barely transparent state. "You'll get more transparent the farther you wander from places you had a connection with."

Her lips moved as she committed the rules to memory.

I sneezed. "Well, I'm ready to leave this place," I said, scratching at my nose as we wandered back through the Underground.

Addy's eyes went wide. "Based on all the coughing and sneezing, I think I'm glad I can't smell or breathe."

I froze. "Wait. I never coughed."

Addy's mouth spread into a grim line. "I could've sworn a heard a bunch of coughing right before I found you—er, or you found me."

Fear skittered over my skin. "Addy, that wasn't me."

Had someone else been down here with us the whole time? A shiver walked up my spine, and I turned in a circle to make sure there wasn't anyone behind me. As I turned, my flashlight beam caught on something to our left, something I definitely hadn't noticed the first time we'd passed by that way.

Correction: someone.

"Maybe it was her..." Addy gulped.

A woman lay slumped against a piece of concrete. Her eyes were open, but she wasn't moving. She had that matte look all dead bodies get when their soul is no longer connected to them. She had on a bright orange sundress and a trendy wide-brimmed hat. The scent of sugary peaches stung at my nostrils once more. My stomach turned at the realization that I must've walked right by her. I'd been so excited to see the staircase that I'd been more focused on the exit than my surroundings.

"Hello?" I asked through the knot in my throat, even though I was pretty sure she was gone.

Addy swept past me and inspected the woman. She turned to me, her eyes wide with fear. "She's dead."

Three

My fingers shook as they gripped my phone. I was in the Underground with two dead bodies.

Wait. My phone. I could call for help.

Unlocking the screen, I dialed 9-1-1, keeping the flashlight focused on the woman's body. The display changed, but the call couldn't connect. My gaze flicked up to the service bars along the top corner. I was too far under the streets to get a signal.

"I have to get out of here so I can call for help." My throat felt dry, covered in dust from breathing the stale air down here for so long.

"That's a phone?" Addy stared at the device in my hand, her ghostly head tilting from one side to the other.

I cleared my throat.

"Right." Addy straightened. "You need to get out." To her credit, Addy didn't ask questions as she led me through the darkness, our roles reversing. "You said you came down a different staircase?"

I nodded.

"I don't know where I'm going any better than you, but I'll do my best." Addy shot me an apologetic glance. "Your light was the first I've seen in a long time."

Sadness enveloped me at the thought of her spirit having been stuck down here in the darkness for so long. Ghosts couldn't see if there wasn't any light around.

Addy moved ahead of me, guiding me through the old alleys and condemned first floors of buildings, past her skeleton, straight to the secret staircase clinging to the side of the Morrisey. Leaving Addy behind, I jogged up the steps, pulling in a lungful of the *fresher* air once I was back in the mechanical room. I never thought I'd love the smell of the air in there, but it was a vast improvement over the stuffy Underground.

My call, which had been waiting to connect, finally went through.

"What's the address of your emergency?" the dispatcher asked.

I told her, then explained what I'd found and where. She assured me there were police close by and they would come to investigate.

Pacing in the mechanical room as I hung up, I was surprised when Addy appeared by my side.

"You've been to the Morrisey before?" I stared at her.

"I *have*. They used to throw the best parties in this building. I had a friend who lived here." The way she winked at me made me think he was more than just a friend.

"Then you could've used *this* staircase to get out." A dry

laugh escaped me. "We could've come this way the whole time."

"Yeah, but then we wouldn't have found..." Addy's sentence petered out as she wrinkled her nose.

"True." My throat suddenly felt like sandpaper.

As much as I wished I hadn't been the one to find the poor woman in the orange dress, if it hadn't been me, who would've found her? Would she have turned into a skeleton just like Addy had, forgotten underneath the city for a hundred years?

Addy's ability to set foot inside this specific room intrigued me, and we chatted about the building and what it used to be like back in her day. I learned Addy had more than one *friend* in the building, and she was edging on too much detail about her gentleman callers when the door to the mechanical room opened.

"She should be right over here." Nancy's shrill voice cut through the silence.

My body went rigid. Nancy. I'd completely forgotten to warn her. I'd been gone longer than I should've, gathering the piece of wood for Winnie. Had she come looking for me? If she hadn't before, I'm sure that seeing the police stream into the building would've piqued her interest. She showed them over to where I stood.

"Meg, I—" She clamped her lips shut as she took in the opening in the wall. "Oh, my."

Detective Amaya Anthony, a whip-smart member of the Seattle Police Department, and the owner of hair so shiny she could have a real future in shampoo commercials if she ever tired of the whole crime thing, stepped around the building manager, inclining her head toward me. Behind her was a small group of officers with bags and equipment that I assumed to be her crime scene team.

"Ms. Dawson," the detective said in a flat greeting. "Again, so soon?"

I contorted my face into an apology. "Sorry."

It hadn't even been a week since she'd been here investigating the murder of the man who'd lived in apartment 3B. But there was nothing I could do about that now.

"Here, I can show you the bodies." I gestured to the staircase.

"*Bodies?*" Detective Anthony stopped. "Plural?"

"Well, first I tripped and found a skeleton. When I fell, I must've gotten turned around, and while I was trying to find my way back, I found another, *fresh* body." I immediately wished I'd used a different word.

Taking a deep breath in preparation, Detective Anthony nodded. "Lead the way." She flicked her fingers, motioning for the team of crime scene techs behind her to follow.

"I think I'll stay up here, just in case anyone else arrives," Nancy called, her voice shaking a little.

The detective thanked her, and we started down the staircase. It felt less scary that time, which was ironic because before I had no idea that at least two people had died down there. But I knew what to expect, and having the detective and her group of officers by my side made me feel safer.

"Here's the skeleton." I stopped and pointed to Addy's one-hundred-year-old bones.

Checking to my right, I found Addy standing next to Detective Anthony as she took in the remains.

"This body's been here a long time. Probably before this part of the Underground was closed off for good in the late nineteen twenties." Detective Anthony walked forward to inspect Addy's bones.

"Careful," Addy whispered.

The detective was, of course. She was also quick, mostly because Addy wasn't the reason there was a team of officers with her. Motioning for me to show them to the other body, the detective trailed behind me as we moved deeper into the Underground. It was officially the worst show-and-tell I'd ever been involved in.

"Here's the new one." A metallic taste coated my tongue, proving *new* wasn't much better in the way of word choice than *fresh* had been.

Stepping aside, I let the detective and her team crowd around the body. Now that I wasn't here alone, I studied the woman a little longer than I had before. She was blonde, her hair long and so perfectly curled that she could've been a woman in one of those internet tutorial videos that I could never gain the same results by mirroring. Expensive-looking heels were strapped to her feet and her head was slumped to the side as if she'd passed out, like she might just be taking a nap.

"And you think she used the same staircase we just came down from the Morrisey?" The detective turned toward me, confusion marring her features.

I shook my head. "I seemed to be the first to use that staircase in"—I puffed out my cheeks—"decades, at least. It was blocked off with those pieces of wood. There's another staircase over here, that leads out to the alley, but it's locked."

A question flashed behind Detective Anthony's eyes, as if wondering how I knew where it led if it was locked.

"I'm guessing, based on where we are under the block," I added quickly.

A muscle in her jaw jumped. "Would you show me?"

I led her over to where Addy and I had found her first exit. The detective checked the door even though I'd told her it was locked. Her lips thinned into a frown, and she turned back. Once we'd returned to the scene, she addressed her team. "Did anyone find a key on the body?"

A crime scene technician shook her head. "No keys. She has a wallet and a vape device. But that's it in her purse."

"Okay. Will someone go contact the owner of this building and get them to unlock this door for us?" Detective Anthony hitched a thumb overhead.

An officer raised his hand, saying he was on it before he walked off. But once he left, a hushed whisper sat over the remaining officers and techs.

"What?" Detective Anthony set her hands on her hips.

The officers shared a wary glance before one of them stepped closer to the body, moving aside the curtain of perfectly curled blonde hair with a gloved hand. "She also had this stuck into her neck."

A syringe protruded from the blonde woman's neck. The plunger had been pushed all the way down, proving that whatever liquid it had contained was now in the woman's body. I took a shaky step back.

The detective's gaze snapped to me, as if my movement had reminded her I was there. "You didn't see or hear anyone else down here, did you?"

I knew what that question meant. Murder.

"I thought I heard someone coughing at first, but..." I repeated what Addy had told me. The detective still deserved to know. Shaking my head emphatically, I opened and closed my mouth but couldn't seem to convince any more words to come out. I'd been down here with a murderer?

Before the detective could ask me anything else, an officer stepped forward. "You know who this is, don't you?"

The woman narrowed her eyes in lieu of an answer.

"That's Paris Elliott." The words were strangled as they left the officer's lips.

"You're sure?" The detective placed a hand on the rundown wall next to her.

If I didn't know better, I'd say she needed help standing. But Detective Amaya Anthony was tougher and more competent than anyone I knew. Well, besides ... Nancy. Oh, gosh. And she'd just about lost control of the building today during the meeting. It seemed as if all my metaphorical rocks were crumbling around me today. If that wasn't bad enough, Addison rushed over to me.

"Did she say *Elliott*?" Her already pale, ghostly features turned downright ashen. "But ... that's *my* last name. Elliott." She jabbed a thumb toward her chest. Whirling around to look at the body, Addison whispered, "She's ... Is she related to me?" The question caught in her throat.

"This is bad." Detective Anthony raked a hand over her face, and it took me a moment to recognize that her statement wasn't in response to what Addy had just divulged.

"How so?" I ventured to ask.

The detective jumped, having obviously forgotten I was

there. "Oh, the Elliotts ... well, they're just a family we have *a lot* of experience with. A lot," she snapped at an officer nearby. "If an Elliott is dead, I need you to round up all the Stimacs. I need alibis. Double—no, triple-check each one."

The officer started to protest. "But, we don't even know for sure it was mur—"

"People don't stick needles into the backs of their necks," Detective Anthony snapped. Seeing the officer recoil, the detective softened and added, "The Elliotts are going to demand it, regardless. I'd rather be prepared."

Everyone jumped into action, a few officers splitting off from the crime scene group.

"The Stimacs?" Addison squeezed her eyes shut. "Why would she think they've got anything to do with this? They were our best friends."

Detective Anthony moved off, but the officer she'd been talking to remained next to me, pressing her fingers to her temples like she was overwhelmed. Her badge told me her last name was Morton.

"Excuse me." I sidled closer to her. "Why did the detective say that about the Stimacs?"

Officer Morton glanced over at the detective and then leaned closer to me. "The two families have been feuding for, like, a century. It's the closest thing to the Hatfields and the McCoys I've ever experienced."

"They've killed each other before?" I blinked in surprise. I wasn't well-versed in the infamous Hatfield and McCoy feud, but I thought I remembered there being deaths on both sides.

Officer Morton tilted her head. "Allegedly. Though we haven't ever been able to pin anything on either side."

Addy drifted away, mumbling something to herself.

I watched her go, then turned back to the officer. "Um, is there anything else you need from me, or..." I drifted toward the staircase that would lead me back to the Morrisey.

Officer Morton checked the clipboard she held, full of notes. "You're good to go. The detective knows where to find you if she has any more questions."

Thanking her, I ducked over to where Addy paced in the corner. Well, paced wasn't exactly the right word. She floated in a line, back and forth.

"Come with me," I whispered, jerking my head toward the staircase. I wanted to make sure she was okay, but I couldn't have a conversation with a ghost around all these cops.

Addy followed as I scaled the secret staircase back up to the Morrisey's mechanical room. Nancy was over by the door to the lobby, ushering in more police. I ducked around the furnace so they wouldn't see me. Addy could've gone into the lobby if she'd been to the Morrisey while she was alive, but there would be much less privacy out there, and I wasn't sure if she could go to my apartment. This was the safest place to talk. The hum of the furnace whirred in the background, creating a white noise that calmed me after the suffocating quiet of the Underground.

"Are you okay?" I asked, trying to meet Addy's gaze, but her eyes were still focused on the floor, her head hanging forward in a manifestation of depression.

"It makes no sense," she muttered, then glanced up at

me. "You said it yourself. I was so close to solid here because my family's store was nearby. Well, we owned the building with the Stimacs. The place was practically my home. What changed?"

I shrugged. "A lot can change in a hundred years. Though, it sounds like they've been fighting for close to a century, so maybe something big went down after you died." Eyes widening, I said, "Or your death started the feud. Do you think a Stimac could've been responsible for you being down there?"

"Absolutely not." She spat out the sentence and shot me a glare. Then she blinked. "But that doesn't matter anymore. What matters now is that someone in my family just died." She held a hand out toward the staircase to the Underground.

Thinking about that, I asked, "You're *sure* you didn't see or hear anything happen? Other than the mystery coughing, that is." That had to have been the woman in orange, right? Or had it been the murderer?

Addy's teeth raked over her bottom lip as she thought. It looked like she was thinking hard—and that wasn't an insult. She really did seem to be racking her brain for details. After a few moments, she said, "There was so much darkness and quiet for so long. Then I heard the coughing. I went searching around, and that's when I found you. I didn't look anymore because I thought it had been you."

Sighing, I said, "Detective Anthony is good at what she does. She'll figure out who did this to your relative, I'm sure."

Addy bowed her head in a half-hearted nod.

"Okay, well ... I should be going." I checked my watch.

"Have fun." It didn't sound possible anymore, not with everything we'd just learned.

Addy didn't move.

"Hey," I said softly. "I thought you couldn't wait to explore *your city* now that you're free?"

She fiddled with her sparkly dress. "After learning about this feud, though, I guess I don't feel like being alone."

I hesitated, not because I wanted to kick this poor ghost out into the city by herself, but because things were currently not the greatest with the other ghost in my life. Ripley wasn't herself right now. I wasn't sure if this bubbly party girl was ready for the brooding grunge soul in my apartment. I also wasn't sure Addy was what was best for Ripley at that moment. My ghostly best friend had a strong hatred for all things peppy at the best of times.

But as I glanced over at the flapper girl next to me, *peppy* didn't seem to describe Addy anymore. Ever since she'd learned the identity of the woman in the orange dress, she'd seemed just as sullen as Ripley had been lately.

Maybe they'd be perfect for each other, after all. I decided they would have to be because Addy was staring at me like a lost puppy, and I was out of ideas about how to help Ripley.

It wasn't the first time she'd suffered from depression. Her birthday, the anniversary of her death, the day she'd learned that her family had moved away and she couldn't follow because of her tether to me, all of those things made her temporarily miserable. Each time, she took her frustration out on me, needing to fix something in my life—broken or not—to kick her out of it.

The thought that Addy could be her project this time instead of me was too appealing.

"You'll have to excuse my ghostly friend upstairs. Ripley just went through a brutal breakup."

Breakup was a wholly inadequate way to describe what Ripley had been through. I wasn't trying to belittle what my friend was feeling, but it was a long story, and Addy was already dealing with a lot of her own.

Luckily, the word breakup seemed to be all Addy needed to hear, because she nodded seriously and followed as I walked into the lobby.

I waved to the small group of residents gathered there, but my neighbors were busy trying to calm Winnie Wisteria, who was upset about—well, I wasn't sure if it was about yet another body being found, or because it would have to take precedence over closing off her passageway. Whatever the reason for her distress, she created enough of a distraction that no one rushed over to speak to me as I emerged from the mechanical room. Taking advantage of the distraction, I slipped into the stairwell and started up to the fifth floor.

As I climbed, I listened for signs of other residents in the stairwell. Normally, I wouldn't chance talking to ghosts in such an open area. The stairs echoed like nobody's business, and I'd made too many mistakes thinking I was alone, only to find that someone had heard me having a conversation "with myself." But Addy's countenance seemed to droop more with each step, and I felt the need to get her mind off what we'd just learned.

"So, you went to a lot of parties back in your day?" I asked, condensing the hints she'd been giving since we met.

Eyes brightening for the first time in minutes, Addy nodded. Without further questions from me, she launched into a list of her favorite local spots. It sounded like the girl had been out every night of the week, going to one speakeasy or another. With each floor, Addy's spirits grew. Talking about her life seemed to kick her out of the sad state she'd been in downstairs.

As we climbed, Addy also grew slightly more translucent, making me worried she wouldn't be able to enter. Which was why I stopped at the entrance to the fifth floor and flicked an eyebrow up in a silent question directed toward Addy. She walked forward, letting me know she'd been on the fifth floor before, per the ghostly rules. I performed the same check as I stopped in front of apartment 5A and unlocked the door.

I didn't know whether to be disturbed by the wink Addy gave me next or ask about the story behind it, so I pushed my way inside.

Seeing Ripley moping as she glared out the window at the people walking through Pioneer Square was something I would never get used to, regardless of it having been the sight I'd come home to for the past few days.

"Hey, Rip," I whispered.

Sure, the guy I liked was in Japan for the foreseeable future, having left before I could tell him how I felt about him. But the pain we were going through wasn't the same. Laurie would be back someday. Clark was gone forever.

She didn't even check over her shoulder.

"I, uh, met a new friend."

Ripley still didn't move.

Desperate for something that might help raise my

friend's spirits, I glanced at where Addy stood next to me. Her fancy dress caught my eye. Our recent conversation about all the parties she used to go to certainly seemed to have picked up her spirits. Maybe it would help Ripley too.

"Okay, that's it. We're going out." I cut the air with my flat palm.

Ripley stayed put, but Addy clapped and jumped up and down. "Oooh! Yes. I haven't been out in ages."

Four

At the sound of Addy's voice, Ripley finally turned around. Her forehead, already scrunched in anger, wrinkled further in confusion.

"Hi, there! Ripley, is it? I'm Addison. Nice to meet you." Addy glided forward, hand outstretched.

About halfway to Ripley, Addy slowed, and her hand curled back toward her body as she noticed Ripley's dark eyeliner, dyed red hair with dark roots, and her Seattle grunge attire. A small *oh* escaped her lips, but she forced her hand back toward Ripley and fixed her smile back onto her face. "You can call me Addy."

Ripley just stared at the woman's outstretched hand.

"You can't touch anyone, Addy," I whispered. "Remember."

The ghost sputtered out into a laugh. "Oh, right. I promise I'm not actually new to this whole ghostly thing. I just haven't been around another soul in a century."

"You don't say," Ripley answered before turning back toward the window.

"It's a funny story," Addy supplied, even though Ripley hadn't asked. "I thought I was stuck with my skeleton, but it turned out I was just trying to leave in all the wrong spots." She let out a light giggle. "I didn't know the rules about going places I'd been while I was alive, but Megs here helped me out."

At Addy's use of Ripley's nickname for me, my ghostly best friend's gaze shot back around. She looked the new ghost up and down, as if seeing her for the first time. What really got her attention, however, was when Anise, my tiny black kitten, galloped over from where she'd been sunning herself in the window.

Her green eyes locked on to the area where Addy stood, and she seemed to follow the sparkling beads dripping from Addy's dress as they danced in the light. We all stared at the kitten for a moment before she meowed, jumped three feet in the air, and then skittered off to the loft where my bed was located.

We all seemed to shake our heads in tandem, confused by the interaction.

Ripley strode over to Addy. "Wait. How'd you meet Meg?" she asked, getting closer to the new ghost than she strictly needed to.

To her credit, Addy didn't budge.

Jabbing a thumb toward me, Addy said, "Meg found my bones downstairs."

Ripley's attention cut to me so aggressively that I put my hands up in defense, as if her look could actually slice me.

"Hey, you decided not to come to the meeting." I explained how I'd been texting with Laurie and had accidentally volunteered to help Nancy.

"You texted Laurie?" Ripley stepped forward.

"Who's Laurie? He sounds delicious." Addy's shoulders pulled up with excitement as if she were excited to dish about boys.

That reminded me I still hadn't texted Laurie back. But the amount I would need to fill him in on, added to the two ghosts in my presence, told me it would have to wait.

I nodded to both of them. "But when I went to find the piece of wood Nancy needed, I found a secret staircase to the Underground, which is where I stumbled on Addy's…" I petered out, not sure how to describe her skeleton right in front of her without feeling crass.

"My bones," she whispered, eyes alight, her tone holding excitement rather than worry.

"And another … more recent … body." I grimaced, trying out yet another adjective for the woman in the orange dress.

"She's related to me," Addy explained, but the excitement of meeting another ghost seemed to have bolstered her mood enough that the reminder didn't send her back into the sadness she'd been experiencing downstairs.

Ripley blinked like she was coming out of the fog that had encased her since Clark left. "Wait. Start over. *What?*"

We repeated everything, using considerably more detail the second time now that Ripley seemed ready to listen.

"Another body in the Morrisey?" Ripley's lips parted in surprise.

"Bod-ies," Addy corrected her, but then she turned to me. "Another?"

Sitting on the couch and folding my legs under me, I said, "We just got through a separate murder investigation in the building." Knowing the police were handling the murder of the woman in orange, I focused on Addy. "So, you don't remember anything about your death?"

The question was merely a fail-safe. I *knew* spirits usually couldn't recall the exact scenes of their death. It was another way Ripley was atypical when it came to ghosts; she could relive the exact accident that had killed her—including details like how many times she'd asked the greasy-haired boy who'd been driving to slow down, or the squeal of tires on wet pavement—anytime she wanted. And after hearing about how Ripley constantly replayed the accident in her mind, I could see why most ghosts didn't have access to those memories, knowing they would just obsess over them.

But because Ripley was an exception, I needed to make sure Addy wasn't as well.

Addy's gaze traced the ceiling of my apartment as she thought. "Everything was so dark down there for so long, I..." Her words petered out. "I do remember there being blood." She nodded as she became more and more sure about that fact. "Yes, when there were lights back then, before they shut everything up, I remember there was blood. I also remember they didn't see me. I kept yelling at anyone who walked by, trying to tell them I was there, but they couldn't hear me because I was just a spirit, and they didn't see my body tucked back in that closet."

"What did you mean when you said they shut everything *up*?" I asked.

Addy hunched her shoulders and lifted her hands. "By the time I appeared as a spirit, it seemed like they were in the process of closing it up tight. Then there was nothing for so long. Until today with that woman coughing and then your flashlight."

"And you just stayed there for a hundred years?" Ripley asked flatly.

Addy's small shoulders slumped forward. "I tried to leave at first, but then I figured I was stuck there as some sort of punishment for how I'd lived."

Intrigued, Ripley's brows twitched. "And how was that?"

Any sadness seemed to leave Addy momentarily. Her eyes glittered with memories. "So much partying. Drinking, smoking, dancing, men. A lot of men."

Ripley smiled for the first time that week at Addy's last addition.

"People always told me it would catch up with me." The sadness returned to Addy's posture. "I thought that's what had happened, that I was stuck in that awful place as a consequence. So, I shut down. It's why I didn't notice more about whatever happened to that poor girl. I wish I could be more helpful."

I looked from the already depressed Ripley to the now depressed Addy and let out a heavy sigh. Oh no. I was losing them again. We needed to get this show on the road. The amount of light I'd seen return to Ripley's eyes in just that brief conversation gave me hope, and I wasn't going to give it up.

"So ... what do you two say about going out? Should we hit a bar or a club?" I wasn't one to frequent clubs, but I figured Sunday evening at dinnertime might not be too crowded.

Addy's eyes lit up. "Yes."

But Ripley was harder to convince, it seemed. "You hate going to clubs." She watched me suspiciously.

"I don't *hate* it." I wobbled my head from side to side. "Plus, you love them, as does Addy, apparently, and this is all about cheering up the pair of you."

Conceding, Ripley asked, "Where should we go?"

Addy squealed. "I know just the place! I hope it's still around. Follow me."

I changed into clothes that weren't covered in dust from the Underground, and we followed Addy downstairs. But instead of taking us deeper into Pioneer Square, toward the trendier bars closer to the sports stadiums, she turned left on the same block as the Morrisey and held her hands out like she was showing off a prize on a game show.

"The dive bar?" Ripley and I asked, shooting dubious glances at one another.

"This is the building my family used to own. Come on!" She urged us forward, only momentarily balking at the neon advertisements in the windows and the faded signage before disappearing through the grimy door.

The Square was around the block from the Morrisey and had been there for as long as I could remember—Ripley, too, if the scowl on her face was any indication. It was one of those places where the choice of black paint had more to do with the need to cover up a century of grime and dirt rather than wanting an edgy aesthetic. I'd been too young before I left for the East Coast to visit the place, but I'd had no compulsion to do so once I'd returned a few weeks ago.

Even though we'd collectively known the spirit for less than an hour, Ripley and I followed Addy into the Square, hoping for the best.

It took a moment for my eyes to adjust to the darkness inside the building, having been used to the brighter July sunshine outside—even with evening clouds rolling in and covering the sun. There was only one customer sitting at the bar, and a middle-aged bartender stood behind the counter.

On the bright side, the place was about as far from a club as we could get. I wouldn't have to worry about crowded dance floors or long drink lines here. No, this was the place people went to drown their sorrows after a messy divorce or after getting laid off from their job.

Addy stood frozen just inside. For a moment, I wondered if she saw the same sad picture Ripley and I did. But as I stepped forward, I realized that a look of awe filled her expression.

"Are they serving *alcohol* here? Out in the open?" She scrunched up her shoulders as if the thought scandalized her.

I couldn't speak without drawing the attention of the bartender and the one customer, so Ripley answered for me.

"Yeah." She placed a hand on her hip. "What else would they serve?"

And then it hit me. Addy was from the twenties. "Prohibition," I whispered to Ripley.

Her eyes went wide. "Oh, they repealed that," Ripley told Addy. "What used to be here?" she asked Addy.

"It was a mercantile," Addy whispered, even though she didn't have to.

"Your idea of a fun night out was coming to a ... mercantile?" Ripley scrunched up her nose.

She didn't get a response from Addy, who was entranced. The flapper walked forward, staring at the taps and bottles of alcohol in awe. "I wonder if it's still here."

Not sure what she was talking about, but positive I was going to get odd looks if I continued to stand in the doorway, I slid onto the nearest stool at the bar. I was about to gesture to the bartender for a drink when Addy's gaze landed on something in the corner, and a devilish grin peeled across her face.

"No need to talk to him, Meg," she said. "We won't be here for long."

"What's that supposed to mean?" Ripley crossed her arms over her chest. She was losing patience with this ghost and her penchant for secrecy.

Addy jerked her head to the right. "See that phone in the corner?"

I didn't have to look hard. In the far right corner of the room, toward the back of the bar, an old twenties-style telephone sat on a shelf protruding from the wall. The model had the separate ear and mouthpiece. It would've been precisely what Addy would think of as a phone, rather than a cell phone from my generation, or even the corded version Ripley had grown up with.

I nodded to show her I saw it. Ripley cleared her throat.

"When I say so, you're going to walk over, pick it up, and say the phrase *I'm here to see Jimmy about some fish.*" She whispered the directions, even though no one else could hear her.

"Jimmy? Fish?" Ripley repeated, eyeing me to gauge my reaction.

As ominous as that sounded, I didn't mind the idea of humoring the ghost. Whatever Addy was taking us to see likely hadn't survived a century, and this whole phone thing wouldn't work.

"Now," Addy whispered, her gaze following the bartender as he turned his back on me.

I shot out of my seat and walked over to the telephone. There was no sign telling me not to touch it, as there were next to many other antiques I'd encountered around the city. My fingers closed over the old earpiece, and I picked it up.

Instead of a dial tone, the sound of the phone ringing met my ear even though I hadn't called anyone—not that I would even know how to place a call on that old of a machine.

"Hello?" a woman answered after a few seconds.

Leaning close to the mouthpiece, I blurted out the phrase. "I'm here to see Jimmy about some fish," I said as quickly as I could while I checked over my shoulder.

The bartender watched me. My spine stiffened. I waited for him to walk over and stop me, but he didn't budge. In fact, he went back to unloading the small dishwasher behind the bar as if he saw people talking on the antique phone all the time.

In my ear, the woman on the phone said, "Um ... I'm sorry. What name is your reservation under?"

Frowning, I wet my lips. "Reservation? I don't ... have one."

There was a beat of silence on the other end of the line. Then she said, "It's early, and a Sunday night. I think you're fine. Come on down."

The antique wooden walk-in-cooler door in front of me, that I thought had just been one of the bar's walk-in refrigerators, clicked. I shot a glance at Ripley before pulling it open. Addy, grinning like the Cheshire cat, walked through first. A dimly lit staircase led down.

Not another staircase, I thought to myself. But the sound of soft electronic music and the clinking of glassware pulled me forward. The cooler door closed behind me. I started down my second secret staircase of the day, hoping this one held fewer bodies—preferably none, actually.

In contrast to my first staircase, instead of getting creepier and the smell mustier, things got more interesting and a pleasant vanilla odor grew as I descended. Warm yellow lights in tasteful wall sconces lit the way down.

The staircase spit me out into a room that held a long bar and five tables. Two of the tables were small, intimate two-seaters. Four or five chairs surrounded the other tables to accommodate larger parties. The lighting was low and the décor reminiscent of the Roaring Twenties. Black-and-white photographs adorned the walls, and many of the chairs appeared to be antiques from the era as well.

A woman about my age with a nose ring and dark brown hair lifted her chin as I entered. "I can put you over in the corner by the mirror." She swung her elbow out to the right so she didn't have to put down the glasses she was prepping.

Ripley walked immediately ahead of me with her arms out in a ready stance, as if she could take the brunt of any traps or surprises I might encounter.

It didn't take me long to realize what I'd walked into. "It's a speakeasy," I whispered, more to myself than anyone, but Addy turned back and nodded, her eyes sparkling along with her dress in the dim lighting.

A card-stock menu on the table the bartender had directed me toward confirmed my suspicions. It told me I was in The Cooler, a speakeasy that had been around since Prohibition. While the space upstairs had obviously turned from a mercantile to a bar in the century since Addy was around, this place had remained.

The information card also explained that they had no formal menu, but that a bartender would come by to ask me what flavors I liked so they could create a custom cocktail for me. I had to hand it to my new ghostly friend. This was miles better than a loud club.

"Addy, this is really cool," I whispered behind the information sheet.

There were only two chairs at my table, so the ghosts simply floated across from me.

Addy studied the bar. "It's a little different than it used to be, but I spent a lot of time here back in the day. Why *is* it still here if alcohol isn't illegal anymore?"

"People love secrets, and the idea of a speakeasy is fun," I said. "It's like a treasure hunt and a night out all in one."

Addy seemed to consider the idea, but next to her,

Ripley's eyes went wide as she focused on something over my shoulder.

"I'm sorry, did you say something to me?" the bartender asked, having come up behind me.

My cheeks turned red as heat flushed through my face.

Five

My throat felt hot. How much had the bartender heard of my ghostly conversation?

"I, uh, was just talking to myself," I said, flinching prematurely as I waited for the inevitable teasing that usually followed such an admission in my past experiences.

Instead of mocking me for my odd behavior, the bartender simply shrugged. It wasn't so much out of acceptance, but more a lack of interest. Her expression was passive, as if she couldn't care less who I talked to, as long as it wasn't her.

"So, what can I get you?" she asked, pulling out a notepad and pen. She inclined her head toward the information sheet I was reading. "Did you have time to look that over?"

"Yeah. No menu. I just tell you what I like."

"That's pretty much it," she said, poising her pen above the notebook to show me she was ready.

"Well, I don't drink a lot, but my aunt's favorite drink was always a French 75." I remember thinking it seemed so classy any time Penny would order one.

"A classic prohibition-style cocktail." She bobbed her head. "Gin is a great spirit to start with. Do you want to incorporate some sparkling wine too?"

I considered the question. "We can keep it simple and just stick with the gin."

"Cool. And what flavors do you like? Citrus, savory, smoky?" She listed some options.

My eyes lit up at the first. "Citrus is great. I like tangy things. And sweet things."

She tilted her head with interest. "Like fruit forward?" When I nodded, she listed some fruit flavors. "Peach? Berry? Passionfruit?"

Her mention of peach made my stomach tighten as I remembered how the dead woman had smelled so strongly of artificial peaches. No, I didn't think I'd want anything peach flavored today. Berries were always good, but I sucked in a breath at the last one. "Yes, passionfruit is one of my favorites."

The bartender tapped her pen against the notepad. "Gotcha. I'll get started on that right away. I'm Zoe, by the way." Her offer of a name felt more like a customer-service consideration rather than a friendly gesture, though, based on the apathetic way she said it.

"Thanks, Zoe."

I turned my attention back to the information sheet, reading over a little more history about the business above. It all matched up with what Addy had told us. It had been a mercantile back in the early days of the city, changing midcentury to the bar it was now.

After a few moments, however, Zoe's movement behind the bar became more interesting than building history. She looked like a mad scientist, pouring, measuring, shaking, and fiddling with the presentation. Even the ghosts were mesmerized as they watched her work.

Minutes later, Zoe brought over a delicate cocktail glass filled with a frothy liquid.

"Okay," she said after she set the drink in front of me. She pulled the notepad out of her apron and read off the front. "This has gin, passionfruit purée, lemon juice, and an egg white for the froth, plus some bitters on the top."

I took a sip, smacking my tongue as I appreciated the delicate balance between sweet and sour. "I think that's the greatest thing I've ever tasted."

Zoe nodded proudly and seemed like she was about to leave when she paused and shot me a sidelong glance. "Can I ask you a question?"

I dipped my chin as I took another sip of my drink.

"What brought you here tonight?" She fixed me with a questioning stare. "I mean, you seem like you've just stumbled onto one of the more well-hidden speakeasies I've ever worked at. And what was that phrase you said instead of telling me your reservation name?"

My gaze jumped over to the ghosts, but I realized I didn't need their help. "I'd heard that this used to be a real speakeasy during Prohibition times. The phrase I said was what they used to say to gain access. I didn't know if it was still in use." Jabbing my thumb over my shoulder, I said, "I live in the Morrisey. I just moved back after years away, and I'm finally old enough to drink here, so I thought I'd check it out."

"The Morrisey? You live there?" Zoe warmed considerably. She pulled up a stool and plopped down.

Ripley's gaze narrowed at the change in the bartender. If this had been New York, I would've shied away from the small talk, but I was trying to unlearn some of the things I'd decided about myself over the past few years. Contrary to what I'd thought in New York City, I did want to be an artist, after all. And I was working on being more open to talking to new people, even though I'd avoided it during my time in the bigger cities.

"I grew up in the Morrisey, actually." A wide smile eased over my lips. "But I've been on the East Coast for a while."

"Shut up. That's where I'm from." Zoe swatted my arm. "I grew up in Vermont."

She'd gone from treating me like a customer to a long-lost friend. I pushed past the questions in my mind about why and said, "New York and Chicago, for me. What brings you here?" I took another sip of my drink.

It was surprisingly comfortable talking to Zoe. The only thing lacking was for Zoe to have her own drink while we talked. But at my question, Zoe's expression fell, and it seemed I'd killed the good mood we'd both been in.

"Oh, sorry. That's nosy of me." I waved a hand to dismiss my question. "You don't have to answer."

She laughed, but it was tight and humorless. "No, it's okay. That's a completely normal question. I'm the problem." There was a moment of tight-jawed silence before Zoe said, "The thing is, my mom just died about a year ago. I needed to get away."

Instead of giving her a pity tilt of my head as I'm sure most people would have, I set down my drink and blurted out, "*My* mom's dead too." Heat raced to my cheeks once again, and I got ready to be wholly embarrassed by my reaction.

But Zoe didn't make me feel weird. In fact, she leaned forward and said, "Get out."

I shook my head. She couldn't get me to leave now if she paid me. "I mean, my mom died when I was born, so I never knew her. I'm sorry you lost yours."

"Thanks," Zoe said. "I never met my dad, or any family, for that matter, so I'm floundering a little and kind of searching for my place in the world." This version of her was so different from the aloof, distant person who'd taken my order. The woman sitting in front of me was warm, and genuinely seemed interested in hearing my story.

Which was why I sucked in a breath and said, "This is *so* weird. I don't know who my dad is either."

"Are we the same person?" Zoe smacked the side of her barstool.

Ripley snorted, but I ignored the negativity radiating from her.

Since it seemed like I didn't know what to say, Zoe added on, "Well, we're the same other than the fact that you live in an awesome building, and I'm literally living out of boxes in a rented room."

Finishing my drink with a satisfied smack of my lips, I thought back to our building meeting earlier, and Nancy's first agenda item. "You know, there's actually an apartment available on my floor. If you're interested in being my neighbor."

Zoe's eyes flashed with interest, but then the door at the top of the staircase closed and footsteps rang through the small speakeasy. Two handsome men who were probably a little older than me came down the stairs. The one who appeared first had longer hair, the dark tips of which skimmed over the tops of his ears. He had a full beard and looked like he should be fighting paranormal crimes on some kind of television series instead of here in this bar. The man who followed behind him was similarly good looking. His hair was shorter and lighter. Instead of the self-assured air of the first man, the shorter-haired one looked a little panicked, like someone was chasing after him.

Zoe checked over her shoulder. "Well, those are my bosses. I'd better get back to work. Let me know if you need anything else." She patted the small table in front of me and then tucked the stool back where it had been under the bar.

"That was weird, right?" Ripley asked.

But Addy was too busy staring at the handsome men to answer Ripley. "Those are her bosses? Lucky girl."

Ripley didn't add to Addy's ogling, an unusual occurrence since talking about cute guys was one of her favorite pastimes. Her gaze fell to her hands. Right. Clark. Talk of handsome men wasn't helpful right now.

I left cash on the table and waved to Zoe in thanks as I walked toward the staircase. But as we climbed the stairs and walked out onto the street outside the Square, Ripley surprised me by asking where we wanted to go next.

"I think I'm going to head back, actually. I've got that painting to finish," I said, knowing she wouldn't give me a hard time if it meant I was working on my art.

But it didn't matter because Addy was all for the idea. She had a list of places they could try next, and Addy chattered at Ripley as they walked off into the balmy evening.

Walking back into the Morrisey, questions piled up in my mind when I didn't find the Conversationalists in their normal place in the chairs directly to the right of the entrance door. Darius, Art, and the ghostly addition of George, were our resident chatterboxes. They sat in the lobby most of the day, treating it as a social club of sorts.

As I stepped farther inside the lobby, the mystery of the missing Conversationalists was not only solved, but quickly became the least of my problems. A small crowd was gathered between the mailboxes and Nancy's apartment.

That was when I spotted the Conversationalists. They were positioned between Nancy and a small mob of people who were pointing and yelling. Tiny Opal Halifax, our newest resident, was brandishing a sudoku puzzle book like it was a weapon.

Rushing forward, I added myself to the group protecting Nancy. And maybe it was because I'd just spent time with a very outgoing, fun person like Zoe—or maybe it had more to do with people threatening my Morrisey family—but I put myself in between the two groups.

Holding up my hands, I said, "Hey!" The sharp word cut through the crowd.

To my surprise, people actually froze, looking at me to see what I had to say.

"Who are you?" a red-faced man asked from the front of the small, angry mob.

"Meg Dawson." I pushed back my shoulders. "I live here, along with the people you're screaming at. Who are *you*?" I turned the question back on him.

He stifled a brittle laugh. "I'm Foster Elliott, Paris's father, and I demand to know what you people did to her."

"Us?" I jerked my head back in surprise. "We had nothing to do with what happened to Paris."

A woman about my age, with blonde hair that looked remarkably similar to Paris's—just less polished—stepped forward. "You seem to know a lot about what happened to my sister."

My cheeks flared with heat. "I was the person who found her."

"What were you doing down there in the first place?" a different man asked. "Isn't the person who finds the body usually the killer?"

Foster Elliott snapped his fingers. "Write that name down. Meg Dawson. She's going to be the first person we look into after those dirty Stimacs."

Nancy stepped out from behind me. "None of us had anything to do with your daughter's death, Mr. Elliott. I promise."

"Since that part of the Underground is attached to this block, it had to be someone who had access to your building."

I almost mentioned the other way out, where Addy had been able to find an exit, but since it had been locked, I couldn't be sure that was how Paris or her murderer had gotten down there.

"You need to leave now or we'll call the police." Nancy crossed her arms.

A wrinkle cut across the expanse of Foster's forehead as he sneered at the Morrisey's manager. "The police will help *you* with *us* about as well as they'll solve Paris's murder."

Defensiveness for Detective Anthony flared inside my chest. She hadn't always been my favorite, but it seemed we had a mutual enemy in these Elliotts, and I felt the need to protect her just as I had with Nancy and my Morrisey people.

This was getting out of hand. I took out my phone. "Well, just for fun, I'd love to see how the police feel about you storming into our building uninvited."

The older man flung his hands toward the Conversationalists. "They let us in."

Darius and Art cowered. Even George backed into the wall and disappeared.

"Well, we're uninviting you now," I said. "You need to leave."

The small group of them left, muttering curses loudly enough for us to hear as they pushed their way through the lobby and out onto the street.

"Look at our Nutmeg!" Nancy clapped after each word. "She came in like a bulldozer and stood up for us."

Darius didn't seem so excited. "I don't like how they wrote down her name, though. That can't be good."

"Or how that Foster Elliott was glaring at her," Art tacked on.

I let out a dismissive scoff, the high of successfully getting rid of the Elliotts making me feel invincible. "I'll be fine. What are they going to do to me?"

I should've known by the scowls on the Conversationalists' faces, it wouldn't be that easy. I was about to find out exactly what the Elliotts could do.

Six

When I got back to my apartment, adrenaline must've still been rushing through me, giving me courage I didn't normally have, because without overthinking it, I texted Laurie.

> You won't believe how the rest of my day went.

After I sent the message, I did the math and immediately realized it was right in the middle of his workday. Maybe I should've thought it over a little more.

But before I had time to ruminate on it, my phone started ringing. No, not ringing. The buzzing sound of a video call filled my apartment. Laurie's name flashed on the screen.

Accepting the call, my face was mirrored back at me. I couldn't be sure if it was the drink I'd consumed at The Cooler or the adrenaline rush I'd gotten from the altercation in the lobby, but my cheeks had a nice rosy glow to them. Then I became smaller, moving into the corner, as Laurie's familiar face filled my screen.

"Hey," I said through a cheek-cramping smile.

"Hey, yourself." His deep voice seemed to slide through the speaker of my phone, wrapping around me in the most delicious way. "I hope this is okay. I figured it was easier than making you write it all out."

A giddy grin tugged at my lips. "It's great. How's the future?"

Laurie chuckled. "Oh, it's fantastic. We have flying cars and teleportation."

I widened my eyes. "Man, that was fast."

"The Japanese are very advanced." Laurie nodded seriously.

"Well, I'm really looking forward to tomorrow, then." I beamed at him.

"So…" Laurie's eyebrows lifted along with his tone. "I'm dying to know what happened. More building shenanigans?"

"Not even close."

Spotting Anise asleep on the couch, I walked over and joined her, scooping her into my lap. The adorable thing didn't even open her eyes, just snuggled into my arm. I propped the phone on the back of the couch, holding it in place with my free hand.

"I found not just one more body, but two. No one we know, though," I added once I saw the concerned look cross his expression.

I told him all about the secret staircase and the bodies.

"Do they have any idea who the skeleton belongs to?" He took in the story with an extra beat of his lashes.

Congratulating myself for remembering that there was no way I should know the identity of the person attached to the century-old bones and leaving Addy's name out of my retelling, I said, "There were the remnants of a sparkly flapper dress, so I'm guessing they were from the nineteen twenties." I sucked in a quick breath. "Oh, speaking of the nineteen twenties, I went to the coolest speakeasy. It was around during Prohibition, and they reopened again about ten years ago. It's called The Cooler, and it's right around the corner."

"You know, I've heard about that place. I've just never had the time to go, and I thought you had to have reservations."

"I think you do, but I'm good friends with one of the bartenders now, so..." I buffed my nails on the shoulder of my shirt. "I was able to get in without one."

I was so glad we were on video chat so I could see the way Laurie's lips pulled into the sexiest of side smiles.

"Tell me all about it." He sat back on a couch.

Checking the time, I asked, "Are you sure? Aren't you supposed to be at work?"

Laurie coughed. "I am. I *may* have gotten a little cocky thinking that I'd completely avoided having any jet lag, because it's definitely getting me today. I couldn't sleep at all last night. I came back to my hotel at lunch to take a nap because I have dinner with clients tonight."

I opened my mouth to tell him he should use this time to nap, but he spoke first.

"I already tried sleeping, and I just lay there, eyes wide open." He let out a dry laugh. "Talking to you will be a nice break from being frustrated."

"Okay, well, since you're suffering, I'll humor you." I adjusted my phone, placing it on my knee as I jumped into the story. I described the speakeasy, the drink Zoe made for me, and even the list of things she and I had in common.

"Sounds like you had quite the evening," he said when I finished.

Widening my eyes, I told him, "That's not even all of it. When I got home from the speakeasy, there was a full-on *scene* happening in the lobby."

Laurie sat in jaw-clenching silence as I explained how the Elliotts had found their way into the Morrisey and were blaming us for Paris's death.

"Meg, are you sure you shouldn't tell Amaya about this?" His use of Detective Anthony's first name made me squirm a little. Sure, we'd all gotten closer to her after the time she'd spent at the building over the past week, but she hadn't told *me* I could call her by her first name. I was pretty sure that her allowing him to speak to her so informally had more to do with Laurie's hotness and less to do with familiarity.

Swallowing my jealousy, I chewed on my lip. "I will tell her. Tomorrow, though."

"As for the flapper skeleton," Laurie said thoughtfully, "I know someone who might be able to help. My friend Gavin is into all of this Seattle Underground history and he's super interested in Prohibition. He was in my dorm, freshman year, and we all used to call him Mr. Pioneer Square. I swear the guy knows more about that part of Seattle's history than anyone else I've ever met. He might give Amaya a place to start looking for the identity of that body, though I'm sure that case is taking a back seat to the recent death."

Hope sprang up inside me. If Laurie and Amaya were so close, why couldn't he give her Gavin's name himself? The knowledge that he was only talking with and texting me made me happy, and possibly a little smug.

"Sure. That would be helpful. I'll pass the name along."

Laurie's gaze caught on something behind me. "Is that an easel I see in the background?"

I glanced over my shoulder. "Oh, uh, yeah." He'd dropped the news about leaving for Japan when I'd gone over to tell him about my art last week, and I'd gotten sidetracked. "I *may* have started painting again."

If I'd known saying that sentence would earn me such an absolute look of joy from Laurie, I would've started painting a lot sooner. As it was, I drank in the sight of him.

"Meg! That's amazing." His grin only grew more brilliant. "Tell me everything. How's it going?"

"Great. But I think I'm going to have to apply for jobs to support my habit. I dropped two hundred dollars at the art store yesterday."

"Any job or at a gallery?"

I tapped my fingers on the back of my couch as I contemplated that. "I thought about checking out some of the local galleries. Maybe I'll do that tomorrow."

"I'm proud of you, Megs." Holding his hands up, he added, "Not that you *have* to be an artist if you don't want to. I just want you to make that decision on your terms, not because of some jerk in New York."

I chuckled. "I know. And you were right. I missed it. I think working in a gallery for a while would be a great way to make sure."

Laurie ran a hand over his face. "Well, I should probably get back to work. My lunch break's just about over."

"It was nice to see your face." I resisted the urge to look away as I said that. Laurie rewarded me with the warmest grin.

"Same. I think I was missing home more than I was letting on." His lips twitched. "We should do this again."

My heart soared. "I'd love that."

Nodding, Laurie said, "Okay, you call me next time."

"Deal." I lifted my chin.

"Good night, Meg."

"Bye, Laurie."

I hung up, then I hugged Ani to me, squealing into her fur with excitement. What had started as a stressful, awful day had ended on such a wonderful note.

THE NEXT MORNING, I followed through on what Laurie and I had talked about last night. Anise was the only soul there to keep me company as I drank my morning coffee. Ripley and Addy were still out—it must've been a great night.

"Wish me luck, kitten," I said to the little black cat as she stared up at me with her green eyes.

It was another gorgeous summer day in the Pacific Northwest. A cool breeze blew in off the Puget Sound, making me revel in the sunny spots as I moved through the sidewalks snaking through the ornate old buildings of Pioneer Square, and moving toward the gray, more modern, buildings of downtown and Capitol Hill. There were a few galleries in Pioneer Square, but I figured I could end there, hitting the ones farther away from home first thing.

All in all, I stopped by five galleries. One was close to Pike Place Market and had a very cool vibe. The owner had been there and had taken my resume with a smile and a promise that she'd get back to me soon. The next two were tucked into the financial district. They were snootier and reminded me of the galleries I'd worked for in Chicago and New York. Not wanting to unfairly judge them without knowing how they really were—and knowing I needed money regardless—I still dropped off resumes at both.

The last gallery I walked into in Pioneer Square was so weird, I didn't even leave a resume. The owner felt like a carbon copy of Tucker Harrison, my old mentor and the man who'd caused my whole existential art crisis in the first place. But the place right before that, a great little gallery in Occidental Park, was my favorite. It had just as great of an atmosphere as the place in Pike Place, but it would be even closer to home.

Just as with the other galleries, I left a resume with an excited owner, leaving with their promises that they'd be in touch as soon as possible.

After grabbing a coffee and a pastry at the shop on the corner to celebrate a productive day, I returned to the

Morrisey. While there was a hint of unease hanging around the building, walking inside the lobby that morning felt miles better than it had last night. Darius, Arturo—and the ghostly George—were parked at their usual place in the lobby. They waved and called out their standard greetings as I passed.

Opal Halifax had joined them as well, her spindly legs tucked up under her body as she worked on the same sudoku book I'd seen her using to protect Nancy the night before. Speaking of Nancy, the scent of baking bread wafted from the manager's apartment as I walked past and started up the stairs. My legs burned in the best way by the time I reached the fifth floor.

Ripley and Addy were in the apartment when I got back. They were sitting on the floor, playing with Anise. I didn't think twice about that until I remembered they were supposed to be invisible to everyone but me.

"Wait. What?" I pointed between the ghosts and my kitten.

Ripley grinned with all her teeth. "I've always guessed cats could see us. Yesterday, when she stared at Addy, I got to wondering. And then today when we came in, she ran right over and tried to play with Addy's dress."

As if to prove it, Addy gave her torso a shimmy so the beads on her flapper dress moved. She let out a delighted giggle as Anise jumped at her, paws and claws outstretched.

"It doesn't gross you out?" I asked as the kitten passed through Addy's arm, then skidded through Ripley's leg as she tried to stop herself.

Ripley bounced her shoulders. "It feels different.

Humans feel intrusive. Cats kind of feel like a ray of sunshine."

Addy closed her eyes and hummed. "Even though I can't feel it anymore, I'm so glad I can see the sun again."

Ripley and I watched her with similar smiles. I was glad she was free from that dark prison below us. Speaking of darkness, Ripley also seemed to be emerging from the sadness she'd been consumed with. She seemed lighter, and her familiar laugh bubbled out as Anise jumped for Addy's dress again.

"I'm guessing you had fun last night?" I settled onto the floor, creating a triangle around Anise with the ghosts. She trotted over to say hello to me.

Addy and Ripley exchanged a sly glance.

"It was one of the better nights of my afterlife," Ripley said dreamily.

Addy nodded in agreement. "Definitely of mine."

"It's not hard to beat a dark basement." Ripley snorted, teasing her like she did with me. The two of them really were getting close.

I was so happy to see Ripley smile again. The sight felt like my own ray of sunshine on what was already a brilliant morning. It looked like Addy was just what Ripley needed to get out of the funk she'd been in lately. But, just as Rip tried not to be too pushy and excited about me painting again, I didn't want to jinx her good mood by bringing it up, so I just sat with the good feelings for now.

"How was your evening?" Ripley asked.

"Well, when I got back to the building after the speakeasy

last night, Addy's family was here causing a scene," I told them.

"Mine?" She touched her fingertips to her collarbone.

"How so?" Ripley crossed her legs and leaned in closer.

I shrugged. "Mostly threatening us, me especially, saying they think I killed Paris because there was only one way in."

"They don't own that building anymore, I guess," Addy whispered.

Ripley focused on a different part of my story. "They singled you out?"

Wrinkling my nose, I said, "I stood up to Paris's dad, so he told me I would regret it."

"Meg, should we be worried?" Ripley's gaze darkened.

Addy wet her lips. "Yeah, my family was pretty powerful back in the day. I don't know how they are now, but they used to have a lot of ties to the community. I would assume those connections would only grow with time."

I shook my head. "I'm not worried about it. I had a good morning, and I don't want to let it ruin my day."

Ripley's expression softened. "What happened?"

"I applied for a few jobs. Two of the galleries were really cute."

Addy clapped, and Ripley dipped her chin in an impressed nod.

"Dare I say, I think I made a great impression. A few of them said they'd get back to me by later today."

My phone beeped with an incoming email.

"Maybe that's them right now," Ripley said.

I checked it. "Omigosh, it is." Clicking on the email from the gallery by the market, my heart fell.

Meg, I'm so sorry, but we won't be able to offer you a position at this time.

Almost as quickly as it came, another showed up from one of the fancier galleries on Capitol Hill. The wording was almost identical. Before I could even tell Ripley about it, my phone rang.

"It's the gallery I liked the most." I swallowed, composing myself before I answered.

"Is this Meg Dawson?" I recognized the laid-back tone of the owner's voice, the one I'd talked to earlier.

"Yes, this is she." I squeezed my eyes shut, searching for excitement in the woman's tone that might allude to her offering me the job.

"Meg, I'm so sorry, but something's come up, and I won't be able to offer you the position. I just wanted to call and tell you instead of emailing."

Disappointment clogged my throat. Finally, I croaked out a weak, "Oh, that's okay. Thank you for calling."

There was a beat of silence on the other end of the line before the woman said, "I really am sorry. It's just ... no one goes against the Elliotts if they know what's good for them in this neighborhood. My hands are tied."

With that, she hung up. I let the hand holding the phone drop to my side and peeled open my eyes. Two concerned ghosts stared back at me. "She just confirmed that it was Foster Elliott. Because of him, all four galleries said no within minutes of each other." I tried to force a smile but couldn't seem to muster enough happiness.

"I thought that was only three." Addy held up her fingers as she counted.

I pointed to my phone. "I saw one more email come through while I was on the phone. I don't need to open it to guess it's going to be the last gallery."

Addy's neck went taut, and I realized I may have been wrong to dismiss Foster Elliott's threats.

Seven

Frustration about the situation with the galleries wound around me, weighing down on my chest. Despite what I'd just said about not letting the Elliotts ruin my day, it felt very much like it was heading in that direction.

Of course, I wasn't only mad at the Elliotts. I was also to blame. *Why did I tell him my name when he asked?* I berated myself.

Otherwise helpless, I settled onto the couch, scooping Anise into my arms. After her play session with the ghosts, she'd crashed. She barely moved from the small ball she was curled into as I transferred her onto my lap.

Ripley perched next to me, her eyes slitted as she observed me. "I didn't know you were thinking of applying to any galleries." She put a hand on her hip. "When did you make that decision?"

"I can make decisions without running them by you," I

joked, even though almost 100 percent of our history together would prove otherwise.

Addy came over and joined us on the couch. "I've been meaning to ask you two ... how did you get like this?" She flicked a delicate finger back and forth, between us.

Ripley and I shared a look that contained about twelve emotions at the same time. Ours was not just a complicated story, but a sad one. Ripley opened her mouth to explain.

"Rip's my guardian angel," I jumped in, instead of letting her say something untrue about how she was the cause of my mom dying.

My ghostly best friend clamped her lips shut.

"Wait. You're not?" Addy's burrowing gaze traveled back and forth while she tried to read our opposing expressions.

"I make sure she doesn't get into too much trouble since her mom died before she was born." Ripley shot me something between an eye roll and a wink.

Excitement peeled across my face in a huge grin. It was the first time Ripley had refrained from blaming my mom's death on herself. Added to the vast improvement in her mood today, it was huge progress.

Addison scooted closer. Even though it didn't make any noise, I felt like I could almost hear the rustling sound the strands of beads dripping off her dress would make as she shuffled around. "I need to hear every detail."

Ripley grunted as if she'd used up all her energy saying what she already had about the situation, so I took that as my cue to tell the story.

"My mom was nine months pregnant with me when she got into a car accident. A stupid boy"—I glared at Ripley to remind her that it hadn't been her behind the wheel—"was showing off, and he crashed into my mom, killing three of the four people in the crash."

"You were the only survivor." Addy covered her mouth with her hand.

I bowed my head forward. "Ripley's been with me ever since. She has to go wherever I do."

"I *get* to go wherever Meg goes," Ripley corrected, eyeing me the same way I'd just done with her about the car accident. "Whereas you're limited to where you set foot while you were alive, I can go anywhere Meg is ... as long as I don't get too far away."

Addy snapped her fingers. "That's why you said we should stick close last night."

Ripley tapped her nose with her index finger.

Addy squinted. "So, you're like ... best friends?"

Our eyes met and shared smiles lifted the corners of our lips.

"Something like that," Ripley said.

I didn't take her comment as dismissive. She was here in place of my mother, it felt, but she seemed more like a big sister or a protective best friend than a parent. Our relationship was always evolving, too, especially as I grew up and needed Ripley's guidance and protection less and less.

Remembering everything we'd been through together, I softened my attitude toward my ghostly best friend. She'd been right to question my sudden choice to apply to galleries. I would've been surprised if she'd made a big decision without consulting me.

Knowing something that would get us back on the same page, I blurted out, "Laurie and I talked."

"Shut up," Ripley said with a gasp. "Tell me everything."

I did, starting with letting them read over my shoulder as I showed them the text exchange between the two of us. Well, at first, I paused to explain texting to Addy, but Ripley had already done that the night before, so I didn't need to. She simply nodded along as I scrolled through our conversation.

"And then he called me. Well, on video." I squeezed my shoulders up to my ears.

Ripley turned to Addy. "Video is—"

She held up a hand. "We had moving pictures back then." The ghost rolled her eyes.

Ripley did, too, adding, "Her movies didn't have sound, though. You should've seen this one last night. I had to explain just about everything to her. She's pretty well caught up now."

Addy's big doe eyes seemed even bigger as she said, "The future is amazing. Truly, it is. But back to your story about Laurie." She clenched her hands into fists and shook them in front of her body. "I love dishing about boys. I miss it so much."

"Not as much as Laurie misses Meg," Ripley said as she sat back on the couch, almost sinking all the way through it.

I exhaled something that was part laugh, part sigh. "And he even gave me a contact to help with the investigation into Addy's death. His friend from college is really into the Underground preservation and Pioneer Square history. Well, technically, he told me to give the number to Detective

Anthony, but she's got her hands full with the other murder, and I thought *we* could call him."

Addy pouted. "Why do you need him? You've got me. I *lived* through the history."

Ripley tilted her head at me like, *the girl's got a point.*

"Laurie said he knows a ton about the city's history. They called him Mr. Pioneer Square in college."

Addy snorted. "I was alive while Pioneer Square was being built."

"Okay." I turned my full attention to her. "Do you know who might've wanted you dead and why no one found you until now?"

The tip of her tongue ran between her lips. "Okay, well … touché. I don't know any of those things. I doubt this guy is going to know them, either, though."

"Meg, how about we give Addy a shot first? We can do some research and see if she can fill in the blanks for us," Ripley said, then added, "but, if we don't find anything, Addy, then will you let us go talk to this friend of Laurie's?"

I had to hand it to her. It was a suitable compromise.

"Okay. Fine," Addy conceded.

"Good idea," I said. "We have some time now; should we search for information about you?"

Addy clapped her hands together. "Yes!"

Aunt Penny's best friend—and my current neighbor—was a librarian at the Seattle Public Library. And even though Iris was still traveling back from Scotland, she'd taught me enough about which sites to use for research, and I found a single mention of Addison Elliott in an old newspaper article clipping on an Unsolved Mysteries of the Pacific Northwest site. The brief article mentioned Addy had gone missing at the beginning of winter in 1923, and no one had heard of her since.

Seeing we were at a dead end with Addy, I looked up the feud between the Stimacs and the Elliotts. Other than a few articles written about them, many of which had been published in the last ten years, no one seemed to know the reason the feud started.

"You really have *no* idea what happened between your family and the Stimacs?" I turned to Addy. At the risk of repeating myself, I just couldn't believe that there hadn't been any signs leading up to such an awful, long-lasting feud.

A frown line appeared between Addy's brows. "We were all great friends, the last I remember."

"Do you know what you might've been doing down below the Morrisey?" Ripley asked.

"Of course. I loved a ritzy party as much as the next Jane, but I usually ended the night at The Cooler." Addy's gaze dipped to her hands. "It was home."

"If The Cooler was a speakeasy back then, what else was under this block?" I asked. "Like, what was under the Morrisey?"

"Oh, under this building was a big gambling operation." Addy adopted a round-eyed expression of awe.

"You were into gambling?" I asked.

"No." She cut the air with her hand. "I liked a cocktail and to dance. I didn't gamble or anything else." Holding her palm next to her mouth like she was telling us a secret, she added, "I mean, I *tried* getting into the place, but they changed the password nightly, and I could never remember it with all the others rattling around in here." She thunked the heel of her hand against her temple.

"So, you hung out in the Underground a lot? Weren't there a ton of rats?" I asked, remembering hearing that during an Underground tour years ago. "And bubonic plague?"

Addy wrinkled her nose. "There were always rats. We would use our purses as weapons to knock them away from our feet." She gasped. "Maybe I got the plague."

"An outbreak in this area might explain why they didn't find you," Ripley said thoughtfully. "But I really don't think you put yourself in that closet."

Addy cringed. "Probably not."

Tapping my fingers against my lips, I asked, "Did you have any enemies that you can remember? Anyone who might've wanted you dead?"

Shivering, Addy shook her head. "Absolutely not."

Ripley made a throat-clearing noise. "Well, there's only one way to find out."

Addy and I checked with each other, then looked back at Ripley in confusion.

"We need to go down there and help Addy search for clues about how she died," Ripley said. "Maybe something down there will jog her memory."

"The police are already doing that, though. They probably already combed the area," I argued.

"For Paris's death. Sure." Ripley pushed back. "But I doubt a hundred-year-old skeleton is on the top of their list right now. They're going to focus on finding who killed Paris, first."

"That's true," I conceded. "And Addy couldn't really look around over the years because it was so dark. So maybe there is something down there that is important to your case."

Addy gave me a hopeful nod.

"You can show her things in the light." Ripley stood, as if that might convince us to do the same. "I think we should go right now."

I exhaled the rest of my reservations. Detective Anthony and her team might have the Paris Elliott case under control, but we had all the information when it came to Addy's death. They probably still didn't even know her identity.

And while I wasn't keen to get involved in another investigation into someone's death, a case that was a hundred years old seemed fairly harmless. Addy's killer, whoever it was, would be dead, too, by now.

"Well, it's a good thing I didn't get a job today," I said, standing alongside Ripley. "It looks like we're getting involved in Addy's case."

Eight

I wasn't thrilled about going back into the Underground portion of our city block. But having Ripley and Addy by my side made it a little less scary. Also, I'd already stumbled on a skeleton and a body. What was the worst that could happen by going back?

The only tricky part was that I'd returned Nancy's keys to the mechanical room yesterday. I made a quick stop by her apartment on the first floor.

"Hi, there, Nutmeg. What can I do for you?" Nancy dusted the flour off her hands as she stood in the doorway. My feelings about my upcoming trip down to the Underground must've soured my expression because, as Nancy studied me, she asked, "Is everything okay? Did those Elliotts cause trouble again?"

They had, even though that wasn't the reason my face was so tight. But Nancy was almost more protective of me than Ripley was, and I didn't want to worry her, so I kept my news about the galleries—along with my suspicions that it had been Foster Elliott's influence—to myself.

Shaking my head, I said, "Oh, no. I dropped something yesterday, and I was hoping I could borrow your key again so I could see if it's in the mechanical room."

"Sure, doll. Just make sure you don't mess with the crime scene, or that detective will have my head." She rolled her eyes. I didn't blame her for being a little salty about the police presence in the building. They'd already been there enough with the murder in 3B. Added to their time here yesterday, and it was enough to grate on anyone's nerves.

Holding up a flour-covered finger, Nancy moved back into the apartment. She came back a few moments later with clean hands, holding out a single key.

When I stared at the key in confusion, because it differed from the one she'd given me yesterday, Nancy said, "I had to grab the spare yesterday when the police showed up, and you were inside with my set. Once they got the keys from the Stimacs, they used that as their primary entrance, thank goodness."

My breath caught in my throat. "What do you mean, the Stimacs' entrance?"

"The one in that alley right outside their bar," Nancy answered, like it was common knowledge.

Goosebumps formed up and down my arms, creating an uncomfortable pinprick sensation. "They own the Square?"

"And the little speakeasy underneath." Nancy leaned the heel of her hand on the doorframe. "Well, I think they own the whole building, even the apartments above." Unaware of why this information was important, Nancy handed over the key. She placed it in my palm and patted my fingers closed around it. "If you wouldn't mind putting that key back for me after you're done, I would appreciate it." Glancing left and then right, she whispered, "I just tuck it up on top of the doorframe."

I bit back a smile. That was probably the first place anyone would check if they were trying to break in. And as much as I would've liked to think that we were safe in our building, Art and Darius had let the mob of Elliotts in the evening prior.

Taking the key, I nodded dutifully. "I'll put it back when I'm done. Thanks, Nance."

She paused as she was closing her door to offer me a baked good—which I had to turn down since my heart was thrumming with the news she'd just shared, and my stomach was in knots thinking of going down into the Underground once more.

I held up the key and bounced my eyebrows at Addy and Ripley, who waited for me outside the mechanical room door. Even though they didn't have to, they lingered until I unlocked the door and slipped inside, tucking the key into my pocket. I didn't have to worry about moving all the pieces of wood like I had yesterday, but the flimsy police tape crisscrossing the staircase entrance should've been more of a deterrent. I reminded myself that I'd already been down there, and I wouldn't touch anything if I could help it.

"Guess what I just learned from Nance," I told the ghosts as we headed down the staircase. I didn't wait for them to ask before saying, "Your family might not own that building anymore, Addy, but the Stimacs still do." I stopped at the bottom of the staircase, looking back to gauge the ghosts' reactions.

"You don't say?" Ripley said in a singsong voice, laced with suspicion.

Addy's red lips parted. "Wait. Does that mean Zoe's bosses from last night were Stimacs?" She inhaled. "I thought the one with the short hair reminded me of Wally Stimac. I was stuck on that man for so many years. He was as handsome as they come." Addy sighed dreamily.

Laughing, I said, "I was thinking it was more interesting that an Elliott died so close to a building the Stimacs own, but"—I held up my free hand that wasn't holding out my phone and flashlight—"we're here for Addy's case, not Paris's."

Ripley bobbed her head once in agreement, while Addy still seemed to be dreaming of the guy she'd had a crush on. I walked forward, careful to watch my step on the uneven floor.

"Should we start where I found her skeleton?" I asked as we moved deeper underground, whispering even though I knew we were alone—well, I hoped we were.

"Sounds good." Ripley scanned the area.

Nancy had mentioned that the police had used the other staircase as their primary access to the crime scene, so I didn't really know what I would find. I knew they would've removed Paris's body, but I wasn't sure if Addy's remains would still be there.

I was a little taken aback when we found that the closet area where Addy's skeleton had been just yesterday was now completely cleaned out. "Well, the police moved faster on that than I expected."

Addy pursed her lips. "They probably took any clues with them then."

"Not if they don't see something as a clue. You might have better insight. Let's walk around and see." Ripley nodded encouragingly.

As we explored, I kept the flashlight moving, stopping whenever Addy wanted to examine something closer, and the ghosts kept me apprised of where the rats were, so I wouldn't have another run-in with one like I had yesterday.

"This is where that gambling den I was telling you about was," Addy said, wafting a hand toward the closed-off Morrisey basement.

"The one you could never get into," Ripley repeated her words from earlier.

Addy rolled her eyes. "Yeah. The guy who owned the building was a real *pike*."

"Pike?" Ripley asked.

"You know? He's a crook. A real bad egg."

Ripley and I shared a knowing look. We'd heard enough about William H. Morrisey over the past week, specifically the passages he'd designed into the building so he could steal from tenants.

"And the guys he got to work at the gambling operation were even worse." Addy shivered. "He had these terrifying brutes who guarded it like they were keeping government secrets." She held her arms out to signify how large the guys had been. "But the scariest one was the boss. He wasn't as big, but when he looked at you, his eyes seemed to have no light, no soul behind them."

"So why were you trying to get inside if it was so scary?" I asked, thinking of how she'd mentioned she could never remember their passwords.

Her red lips pinched together. "Oh, you know. If it was taboo, I wanted in." She let out a wicked giggle. "Not to mention Wally frequented the place. But it was probably for the better that I never got in because I think my dad would've killed me if he found me in there. And there was no hiding when you were at Morrisey's place. You came away smelling like rosemary for days."

I stopped short. "Rosemary?"

"To keep the rats away ... as much as possible." Addy tipped her head to one side at that last addition to show it wasn't 100 percent helpful. "He tried fresh rosemary and rosemary oil. He even soaked it into the wood."

Ripley belted out a delighted laugh. "Mystery solved."

"Mystery?" Addy asked.

"Yeah, we've always wondered why the lobby of the Morrisey smells so much like rosemary," I explained, and then tacked on a groan. "But without being able to tell them how I know, the residents are going to believe this about as much as we all believe Ronnie Arbury."

Ripley reached forward like she wanted to pat me on the back to show her support. Instead, she just gave me a sympathetic glance and moved on.

"This area was a rival speakeasy, but their bathtub gin

was awful." Addy stuck out her tongue. "Nothing like the stuff my father made." She pushed back her shoulders with pride.

"I thought all bathtub gin was awful." Ripley floated through one of the support beams for the old building.

"Most of it was," Addy explained. "But Dad was a whiz with the botanicals."

"Your dad made it?" I asked. "I thought you owned a mercantile."

"We did. Dad and Elmer Stimac owned the store together. When they had to move up to the second story when the city raised the streets, they were just using the first floor as storage, especially once the city condemned the Underground. But once the ban on liquor started, they came up with the idea to use that space as a speakeasy. Elmer had some old family recipe lying around, but Dad was the one who figured out the process to make it palatable." She turned toward us, moving to lean on the wall but falling straight through it. Giggling, she added, "They made a pretty good team. Dad ran the store and made the gin, while Elmer was the face of the speakeasy." Her smile faltered as she focused on me. "Why do you seem so sad about that?"

"Sorry." I flinched, not having realized that my emotions were so obvious on my face. "I was just thinking that even though all of this is so interesting, none of that helps us with what got you killed or why the two families had a falling out."

"No, *I'm* sorry. I can't think of anything. It was all happy and good." She shrugged. "I had a great life, quick as it was."

"Let's keep going," Ripley urged. "We still haven't made it through the whole place."

We spent the next hour walking carefully through the underground section of our block. Addy told us stories, though none of them led to any further clues about her fate, but it was super interesting to learn about her life and what things had been like in the nineteen twenties.

Slowing as we approached the site where we'd found Paris, Addy said, "I think we'd better tread carefully around here, folks."

Ahead of us was the staircase Addy and I had used to find her first exit. Instead of looking at the stairs, though, this time we were coming at it from the side. Under the stairs was open, looking like a perfect place for monsters—or more rats—to hide out.

Letting my flashlight fall to my side in defeat along with my arms, I huffed—then remembered that I needed the light, and I held it up again. "We've checked, like, every inch of this place. I think I could name the rats at this point."

"Um ... what about that?" Addy held a shaky finger straight in front of her.

Ripley and I had to strain to see what she was studying. But once we did, I could clearly see a door in the scary section underneath the staircase. Well, it was more of a wrought-iron gate, like someone might have in a garden. It was shoved up against the hard-packed earth and stone that made up the raised streets. And even though the enclosed speakeasy was right next to it, there was room for someone to scoot along the passage.

"You think that has to do with your death?" I whispered.

"No." Addy's lips pinched together for a moment. "But it's interesting. I definitely didn't notice it until just now."

"You wouldn't unless you were coming at it from this angle." Ripley moved forward, reaching for the gate before she remembered she couldn't open it, and let out a laugh.

When I reached forward instead, I was sure it would be rusted shut, so I didn't expect any further action than when Ripley had tried. But it swung toward me.

Blinking from Addy to Ripley, I froze. "What do I do?"

"Go through," Addy urged.

Ripley held out a hand. And even though her arm looked solid enough, I would've been able to walk right through it. "Wait. Should you?" She sent a suspicious glare from me to Addy. "Maybe this is how Paris got down here, or her murderer."

Addy frowned. "Right. Good point."

I stepped back and shone the flashlight over the place. "The question is, will this lead us anywhere, or is it just a small gap between the street and the building?"

"What if you just step over the threshold of the gate, and I'll go forward and check things out?" Ripley offered.

Ghostly rules were often confusing, but one we'd been able to figure out was that thresholds seemed to be a big deal with spirits. If I stepped foot over a threshold, that was enough to grant Ripley access to a room.

"It's worth a try," I said.

Careful not to make any noises, I turned sideways and squeezed through. It opened into a tight tunnel that would've been enough to create feelings of claustrophobia in the bravest soul.

Gulping even though she didn't have a body to worry about, Ripley moved forward. Addy and I stood there in rapt silence for a few moments.

Ripley reappeared seconds later, adventure brightening the whites of her eyes. "You've gotta come see this." She scooped the air with her hands.

Scooting through, I felt like the kids in the wardrobe, moving into a different world. But instead of coming out in a frosty forest near a lamppost, I stumbled into a closet. The same trendy music I'd heard playing at The Cooler the other night was piping through speakers. A faint vanilla smell hung in the air.

Brooms and other cleaning supplies took up most of the closet. Placing my ear against the door and listening until I was sure there were no sounds coming from inside, I cracked the door open. Instead of The Cooler, however, the door opened into a small office with a desk and a few chairs. The office in the speakeasy, I realized

Backing up, I walked straight through Ripley, who'd been following me.

"Hey! What gives?" she complained, shuddering as I passed through her spirit.

I shivered at the icy feeling that followed, but I didn't stop.

"What is it?" Ripley asked as she finally caught up with me.

Once I was out of the tight passageway and back in the open Underground, I paced, though it was decidedly harder with the uneven, sinking concrete floors. Addy, who'd been waiting for us out by the staircase, followed me, hoping for answers.

The only one I had wasn't good. "If the Stimacs own that speakeasy, one of them could've easily snuck through that passage to murder Paris."

Nine

After finding that passage connecting the Underground to The Cooler, Ripley, Addy, and I agreed that we needed more background on the Stimacs and Elliotts before we did any more investigating. If they really were like the Hatfields and McCoys, I didn't want to become collateral damage because I'd been looking into Addy's death and had inadvertently gotten tangled up with Paris's.

As per our agreement, Addy admitted we might need some outside help, so she allowed me to contact Laurie's friend Gavin as our next step. Since there wasn't anything online, we were going to need a Seattle history fanatic to find out anything helpful about the feud. I texted Gavin, and he responded, saying he could meet with me the following day during his lunch break.

Luckily for me, I didn't have a job—the Elliotts had made sure of that—and my schedule was wide open. Gavin gave me the address to his office building, which was just a few blocks away from the Morrisey.

"Oh! I can't believe Emmie's is still here!" Addy gaped at a rather run-down diner on the corner as we walked. "My family used to eat here all the time." Addy's eyes glinted as she glanced back at us.

Ripley and I tried our best to appear excited about the old restaurant, but it was harder than I'd expected. Instead, I turned my energy toward locating the place where Gavin worked, only to find it was right across the street from us.

To be honest, the historical society building was a little like the Square. I suppose I'd always known it was there but never really paid attention to it. The plaque marking it as the Historical Society of Pioneer Square blended into the city streets, and I must've walked by it a thousand times throughout my life without giving it a second glance.

Addy, however, seemed to know just what the building was. Recognition flashed behind her brown eyes, culminating in a sparkling smile that made me sure she would be able to enter.

"I need to hear whatever story's behind that look later," Ripley muttered.

Gavin must've been excited because he was waiting for me as I entered the office. Well, I assumed the man with brown hair, a beard, and glasses was Gavin, based on the way his face lit up when I walked through the door.

"Meg?" he asked.

"Hi." I shook his hand when he held it out. "It's great to meet you."

"You too," he said, motioning for me to follow him

down a hallway that smelled like a combination of pencils, an old drip-coffee-machine, and someone's lunch being heated in a microwave. "I haven't talked to Laurie in months." He glanced at me out of the corner of his eye as we walked. "I have to be honest. When he texted me to give me a heads-up I might be getting a call about some remains in the Underground, I expected to be hearing from the police."

Heat tickled the back of my neck. I was hoping he wouldn't know that part, but it seemed Laurie had done his due diligence. Ripley shot me a nervous glance, and Addy tilted her head as if to say *I told you so,* since she hadn't wanted to talk to Gavin in the first place.

Noting my reaction to his statement, Gavin chuckled. "Don't worry. I'm a bit of a sleuth myself, so I understand your inclination to look into this yourself."

The heat climbing up my neck dissipated, and I relaxed as we walked by a few offices. Gavin's coworkers all seemed to have gray hair, I noticed. By the time he showed me into his office at the end of the hallway, I'd say it was a safe bet that he was the youngest person on staff by decades.

His office was small, smelled like old building with a hint of whatever cologne he wore, and was filled with binders and books. He slid into the office chair behind the desk, pointing to a folding chair he'd set up for me on the opposite side. The ghosts wandered, reading the spines of his books and glancing over the papers on his desk.

"So," he said, threading his fingers together. "I'm guessing you're here because of the skeleton they found."

Swallowing to make way for words, I dipped my chin. "I actually found it."

Gavin's eyes shot open. "Oh. Well, I'd love to hear the story behind that."

I explained the whole thing—how I'd found the staircase and stumbled upon the skeleton. Well, the whole thing except the part about finding Paris's body. I didn't want to spill about the Paris Elliott case if word hadn't already gotten around.

"Wow." Gavin busied himself by straightening a stack of papers on his desk. "That must've been scary. And, I take it you have questions about who the skeleton might've belonged to."

I nodded. The way he phrased that made it sound like he was confident he could help me. I hoped so.

"There wasn't much of her clothing left, but it looked like one of those sparkly flapper dresses from the twenties."

Gavin's eyebrows rose with interest. "The Underground was full of illegal activity during that time. It wasn't just Prohibition either. Madame Lou Graham was a master *seamstress,* and she ran an entire group of *seamstresses* who worked in the Pioneer Square area." From the way he emphasized the word and glanced over my shoulder into the hallway, it was clear he wanted me to know those women hadn't been doing any sewing.

He didn't need the code, though. I'd heard about the owner of the largest brothel in Seattle during that time, who'd grown so rich and had donated most of her money to the Seattle school system.

"Is he implying what I think he is?" Addy tapped her foot.

"Oh, I don't think the body was one of them," I blurted,

trying to appease Addy. "Well, I guess I don't have any reason to think otherwise." I shot an apologetic glance over at Addy. "You don't think it has anything to do with the Stimacs and Elliotts?"

Gavin frowned. "Because Paris Elliott's body was found in a similar location? I think that's purely coincidental."

Well, I guess I hadn't needed to worry about whether he'd heard about Paris Elliott's murder.

You wouldn't if you knew the skeleton shared her last name, I thought to myself, frustrated that I couldn't tell him that piece of information.

Unaware of my inner struggles, Gavin continued talking. "The feud between those two is intense. I wouldn't be surprised if it ended in death. I mean, it already has."

"It has?" I angled my body forward. "Other than Paris?"

He dipped his chin. "About twenty years ago, one of the Stimacs was floating in the water near the ferry dock. And a decade before that there was an Elliott and a Stimac who both went 'missing' around the same time. No one ever found them."

"Missing? Is that the first time that happened?" I asked, thinking of the article I'd found listing Addy as a missing person. "Maybe one of your coworkers has heard of something."

It wasn't like I thought any of his coworkers had been alive back then, but I figured if they'd worked there for a while, they might've heard something that could help us.

Gavin scoffed. "Actually, I'm the resident expert on all things involving the feud. It's what I wrote my final paper on during my master's program." He ran a hand through his dark hair. "As for other people going missing ... there was an Elliott who disappeared during the twenties. It was a woman. I forget her name." He snapped his fingers and got out a binder with newspaper clippings, internet printouts, photocopied pages of books, and handwritten notes. His finger trailed down one page. "Addison, that's right. She went missing in 1923."

I worked hard not to let my gaze slip over to Addy as I asked, "Does anyone know why?"

"There are a few different stories floating around. Some say that she ran away with a billionaire and lived the rest of her life on a tropical island somewhere in the South Pacific. Apparently, she was quite the party girl. The men loved her," he added.

Addy waggled her eyebrows. "The feeling was mutual," she purred.

"Others say she was ditzy, and she could've just stumbled into one of Seattle's many infamous gaping holes, though those tended to be drunk men who did that."

Addy's smirk fell at the reminder of that less-than-flattering theory.

"Were the Elliotts and Stimacs fighting then?" I asked, even though I already knew the answer. It was the best way I could think to segue back to the topic.

"No, actually," he said. "That was back when they were all in business together."

"You don't think Addison's disappearance could be the reason the feud started, do you?" I asked, working out a hunch.

But Gavin cut the air with his palm. "No, I know what

started it." His eyes sparkled as he noticed my excitement at his statement. "You see, the Elliotts worked for the Stimacs. It started as a mercantile, but once Prohibition started, they diversified and used their underground area as a speakeasy. Charles Elliott was the one who distilled the gin they served in their speakeasy. Elmer Stimac was the face of the operation, however. He was incredibly charismatic, whereas Charles preferred to stay behind the scenes."

While that checked out with what Addy had told us, I looked to her to make sure the second part about the two partners' personalities was correct.

She reluctantly nodded, but interest shone in her eyes as she listened.

Gavin continued with the story. "The two of them worked so well together that their business relationship was mostly based on gentlemen's agreements. Stimac trusted Elliott with his family's gin recipe, and Elliott trusted Stimac's word that he was part owner of the building they worked out of. The plan, according to people close to the family, was that they would eventually go into business together—if Prohibition ever ended—splitting the gin recipe and sharing the building."

Addy, entranced with the story now, nodded emphatically. Her father must've talked about that.

"Unfortunately for Elliott," Gavin said with a grimace, "Stimac didn't intend on sticking to that verbal agreement about being co-owners of the building. He hid the deed to the building and fired him from the store. In retribution, Elliott started making his own gin using the Stimacs' exact recipe, only he was miles better at it than Stimac ever was.

Well, that's what everyone assumed, since Stimac never tried to make his own to compete. That was where the tit-for-tat battle of theirs started. Once Prohibition ended, the Stimacs were left with the building and the bar beneath. The Elliotts started their distillery, and the fighting has been going strong ever since."

"Elmer fired my dad?" Addy let her dismay show on her mouth. "Why would he do that?"

"Do people have any idea what caused Elmer to fire Charles?" I asked, trying to fill in the blanks for Addy.

Gavin shook his head. "That's one of the big mysteries to this day. It must've been bad to create such a feud, though."

"None of these people even know why they're killing each other?" I spat out the question.

Gavin sighed, giving me as much of an answer as he could.

Addy's whole body seemed to sag with the information we'd learned. She needed a win. I had to keep pushing to see if we could find out more about her death.

"As for this skeleton you found, was there anything else near or on the bones that might help with identification?" Gavin closed the binder he'd brought out about the Elliotts, sure we were done talking about them.

"My handbag was there," Addy whispered. "Next to my body."

Controlling my surprise, and annoyed with myself at not having checked for clues around her bones before the police had taken everything from the scene, I nodded. "There was a handbag next to the skeleton."

"Black beaded with a gold clasp," Addy supplied.

I repeated the information to Gavin.

He tapped a pen on the desk. "Hmm..."

"Oh, no." Addy rolled her eyes. "He's going to suggest I worked in a brothel, again."

Gavin did just that.

"It looked really expensive," I countered, wondering if that would help get him off that line of thinking.

"The women who worked for Lou Graham did well for themselves." He arched a brow.

Seeing I wouldn't change his mind, I worked on expanding it. "Okay, what other options might there be? What other kinds of women with beaded bags might've been in the Underground during the twenties?"

"There was a gambling den down there, under the Morrisey. Well-dressed women would've probably been there, hanging on the arm of the men gambling." He held up a finger. "Though many of them were also—"

Addy groaned.

"Seamstresses," I said flatly instead of letting him repeat it. "Gotcha."

But talk of the gambling operation seemed to spark something in Gavin's memory. Turning toward his shelf, he grabbed a different binder. "Actually, the gambling den might help us with a date on the woman's death." He flipped through a few pages before stopping on one and tapping his finger on a photocopied newspaper clipping. "In 1923, there was a huge police raid on that place. It turned into a shootout, and there were a ton of deaths. Maybe the flapper was shot during that ordeal."

My mind buzzed with the possibility. Nineteen twenty-three had been the same year Addy had gone missing. It was possible. But she'd mentioned that she'd never been allowed in the gambling den.

Wetting my lips, I said, "I found the bones in what looked to be an old closet in the building next to the Morrisey, though."

"She could've gone in there to hide from the shooting, but a rogue bullet might've hit her anyway." Gavin's whole body tensed, like he could see it happening in front of him. His eyes pored over the text on the page. "After that massacre, that section of the Underground was closed off, sealed up."

"That's why everything was being shut up when your spirit appeared, Addy," Ripley said, understanding making her tone light.

Addy blinked as she digested the information. "And why no one ever found me."

Gavin's eyes flicked to the clock on his desk. The motion was quick, discreet, but I caught it. His lunch break was likely ending, and he didn't have all day to answer my questions or follow the probably very loose threads I seemed to want to follow.

I slapped my palms down on my knees like Iris, whose entire family was from the Midwest, had taught me when talking about nonverbal ways to signal the end to a get-together.

"Thank you for talking through that with me. The information about the Elliotts and Stimacs was really interesting. I can see why you're so interested in the subject," I said, standing.

Gavin stood with me, but he didn't move from behind

his desk yet. He watched me with intense interest for a moment before saying, "Let me know if you ever want to talk more. Everyone else I know is completely sick of my obsession with the Elliotts and the Stimacs." He chuckled.

"I will," I said before waving goodbye and heading out.

The ghosts followed at my side quietly, staying silent as we exited the building and stopped outside.

"You won't, though, right?" Ripley said after a moment. "You won't take him up on anything more to do with this feud, right?"

Shrugging, I said, "I don't know."

"But we know how Addy died," Ripley scoffed, adding, "most likely. She probably got caught in that shootout at the gambling den, hid in a closet, and died there." Ripley cut an apologetic glance over at Addy for speaking so unemotionally about her death.

"Then why is she still here?" I asked, getting a weird look from a woman walking past me on the street at that very moment. Wrinkling my nose, I pulled out my phone and put it to my ear so I wouldn't scare anyone else. "If we know how she died, why is her spirit still around?" I repeated.

Ripley opened her palms. "Maybe her unfinished business isn't about her death. Maybe it's that she needs to stick around and have more fun," Ripley suggested, jabbing her elbow in Addy's direction.

The other ghost showed her teeth in a half-hearted attempt at a smile.

"I don't know. I have a gut feeling that we're still missing something. I can't help but think Addy's death is somehow connected to Paris's, to the whole feud. If we figure out one, we might be able to figure out the other." My eyes pleaded with her. "And of the two cases, we know a lot more about Paris's death. Ever since we found that passage into the speakeasy, I've been thinking that maybe we should help look into Paris's death. I mean, I'm kinda friends with Zoe, that bartender from The Cooler. She might be able to get us information about the Stimacs."

Ripley didn't seem to share my optimism. Her scowl deepened.

Inhaling, I said, "Come on. Asking Zoe about her bosses can't hurt."

Ripley crossed her arms. "It can hurt if she's the killer."

The comment came so far out of left field that I snorted. "Zoe? A killer? No way."

"You talked to her for ten minutes while she was at work. You barely know her." Ripley's gaze turned sharp as she looked at me. "You have no idea what she's capable of, let alone what her story is."

"I do. Her story is the same as mine ... practically," I added when my best friend's expression soured.

"Meg." Ripley said my name like I was the most naïve person she'd ever met. "Didn't you catch how uninterested she was in you until she learned you lived at the Morrisey? She gave me Kirsten vibes. The girl wants something from you. Either that or she's hiding something."

My metaphorical hackles raised at Ripley's mention of Kirsten.

"Kirsten?" Addy asked innocently.

I clenched my jaw and crossed my arms, scowling at

Ripley. If she wanted Addy to know, she was going to have to be the one to tell that story.

Shooting me a wary glance, Ripley said, "She was a *friend* Meg made in middle school who didn't have the best intentions. She had no interest in Meg until she learned her aunt was a successful writer. Then she wanted to hang out and kept inviting herself over to Meg's place. She ended up stealing money and some jewelry from Meg's aunt the first time she came over. Meg was too embarrassed to tell Penny, though, so she came up with a different story about how she'd lost the jewelry and spent the money herself."

The story still stung my ego a decade later. As someone who'd been labeled "the weird girl" very early in my school years, I'd been much too excited that anyone wanted to be my friend. And even though I could technically see the parallels Ripley was drawing between that situation and this one, there was one big difference. I was an adult now, not a desperate teenager.

"Yes," I cut in. "But there was also one time with a girl named Jasmine. Ripley was sure she was another Kirsten and tried to convince me to stop hanging out with her."

"Did you?" Addy asked.

Ripley shook her head and rolled her eyes simultaneously.

"I did not." I lifted my chin as I sent Ripley a pointed look. "And she was a great friend, until she moved the next year, but that's beside the point."

Our Jasmine fight had been one of the worst in all the years Ripley and I had known each other. It hadn't helped that it had been during one of Ripley's depression episodes either. Yet another parallel I was drawing in my mind with her feelings toward Zoe, though I would never say that out loud to her.

As if she could tell it was what I was thinking, however, Ripley asked, "So? Why'd you bring up Jasmine?"

"To prove to you that you're not always right, and that I can make my own decisions."

She snorted. "Can you?"

"Yes," I snapped.

Addy chewed on her lip and stared at the ground, looking like she wished she could be anywhere else.

"Fine. If you're so interested in Paris's murder, you and Zoe can figure it out on your own." Ripley spat out the sentence, tacking on the word, "Alone."

"Fine," I barked into my phone.

Ripley spun on her heel and floated in the opposite direction of the Morrisey.

Addy shot me one last worried glance before she followed.

I stomped toward home.

Ten

Because I'd just fought with my ghostly best friend, I didn't notice Zoe as I walked past her on my way inside the Morrisey.

"Meg?" she asked, stepping toward me.

I stopped short. That was weird. I'd just been talking about her—well, more like fighting about her—with Ripley, and then there she was.

"Oh, hey! On your way to work?" I asked, glancing toward the end of the block where the entrance to the speakeasy was. Afternoon seemed an early time for her to start, but maybe she had to get prepped for an evening shift.

Zoe shook her head, and it was then that I realized she hadn't been walking by at all. She'd been standing in front of my building.

"I actually came to see you," she said.

My chin jutted back in surprise. "Me?"

She blew a laugh through her nose. "Don't sound so

surprised. You and I are the same person, remember? You mentioned there was an apartment available."

I'd thought her comment about taking me up on the offer had just been manners. But it looked like she was actually interested. A warning that sounded a lot like Ripley's voice echoed in the back of my mind, but I pushed it away.

"There is," I said. "Do you have time now? Do you want me to introduce you to Nancy?"

"Nancy?"

"She's the building manager. She'll be in charge of reviewing the applications." I crooked a finger so Zoe would follow me inside.

I was used to getting a warm greeting from the Conversationalists each time I entered the lobby. But Zoe and I had a veritable welcome party the moment we stepped inside the Morrisey that afternoon.

Nancy and Opal sat with Darius and Art in the front sitting area. Their eyes lit up, and they smiled as they saw us enter. Opal had a book of crossword puzzles balanced on her lap, though it seemed as if she wasn't getting very far because of the lively conversation they'd been having.

"Nutmeg!" Nancy stood, ushering us over to the seating area and offering the seat she'd been occupying. "Who's your friend?"

"Someone you might be interested in talking to." I gestured to Zoe.

"I'm interested in leasing your open apartment," Zoe said, jumping in before I could say as much.

The residents shared approving glances, liking the fact that she'd spoken for herself instead of letting me be the one to do all the talking. We were a tight-knit building and liked residents who would chat and add to the family rather than hiding away in their apartment. They'd made that mistake with the "Wary McNairys," as they referred to Danica and Dustin on the second floor.

"Color me intrigued." Nancy patted the place next to her on the couch. "What's your name, dear?"

"Zoe Davis." Her shoulders bunched up eagerly, surprising me.

The woman sitting next to me held none of the original aloofness I'd experienced with her in the speakeasy. She seemed to genuinely care about the Morrisey residents' compliments, something I understood. When you didn't have parents, you often searched elsewhere for those parental figures. I'd found them in my Morrisey family, and it seemed Zoe was open to the idea as well.

"Cupcake, Zoe?" Nancy motioned to a plate of brightly decorated cupcakes on the coffee table at the center of the seating area.

Chuckling, she said, "Okay, I feel like *I'm* being convinced to stay here instead of the other way around."

"A friend of Nutmeg's is a friend of ours." Darius dipped his head in my direction, using their nickname for me just as Nancy had a moment ago.

As a girl who grew up without a mother, not knowing her father, there weren't many situations in which I'd been the object of someone else's envy. But at that moment, Zoe stared at me like I was a literal queen, with riches beyond her imagination.

There had been the classmates growing up who thought

it was so cool that my aunt was a famous author and that she gave me so much independence, slippery Kirsten being one of them. But those weren't things I had done or could take credit for. The relationships I had with the people at the Morrisey, however, were those I'd cultivated. I think they would've loved me regardless of my level of interest in them, but I truly saw them as my family and put as much effort into loving them as they did toward me.

Opal slipped out of the black flats she wore, tucking her thin legs underneath her, as she turned to face Zoe as if she were conducting the interview instead of Nancy. "Okay, tell us all about yourself. We're all ears." She rested her chin on a bony wrist and gazed at Zoe. Nancy nodded in agreement.

Zoe blushed under the scrutiny. "Well, I grew up on the East Coast, but my mom passed away last year after battling cancer and"—Zoe cleared her throat like it was clogged with emotion— "and I just couldn't stay there anymore. Everything reminded me of her."

Nancy sniffed. She was a total softy under that tough shell. A loud trumpeting sound came from Art as he blew his nose. Opal reached forward and patted Zoe's hand with hers. Even Darius was tearing up.

Pulling in a deep breath, Zoe seemed to collect herself, and she said, "So, I've been here for about six months, and I've been renting a room from someone I found online, which was fine when I didn't have a job. But now I have a good job and I'm making enough money, and I want my own place. Most of my stuff is still in boxes, so it won't even be hard to move." She lifted her chin like the reality of those positive changes made her very proud.

"Of course you want some space to yourself," Nancy said. "And where do you work?"

"The Cooler, the little bar underneath the Square."

"Oh, right around the corner!" Nancy swiveled her shoulders and shot Zoe a glance out of the corner of her eye. "That's a pretty swanky little place. I heard they don't even have a menu."

Zoe's pride at the compliment shone in her broad smile.

"They do not," I chimed in. "I can attest to that. It's how Zoe and I met."

The Morrisey residents listened with rapt attention.

"What a wonderful meet-cute," Darius said. He was always trying out stuff "the kids say" and inevitably using it wrong, but I loved him for trying.

Zoe and I shared a quick smirk at his misuse of the phrase since we weren't in a romantic relationship, but we let it go.

"Well, I can get started on the paperwork. There'll be a background check, and we'll have to run your credit, but that's strictly official. Unofficially, I'd say you're in?" Nancy posed it as a question, checking with the other Morrisey residents present whose excited postures answered for them.

George, a ghost who stayed mostly in the building lobby, and who'd been floating at the edge of the group, gave me a thumbs-up as he officially approved of Zoe becoming part of the building.

But suddenly there were two more ghosts in the lobby, and one of them was decidedly *less* excited to see Zoe. Ripley stood there, eyes narrowed and chin lifted, the way she glared at people she didn't like. I could practically hear her thoughts. *What's she doing here?* As if I'd been the one to seek out Zoe instead of the other way around. While calling Zoe the moment Ripley and I had gotten in a fight about her would've been pretty low of me, I wasn't sure I wanted Ripley to know that she'd been waiting here for me when I returned either.

Zoe followed Nancy into her apartment to start the paperwork, so I brought out my phone and pretended to take a call while I went over to Ripley and Addy.

"Got something to say about this?" I asked, whispering into my phone so my fellow residents would just think I was on a call.

"You don't think you should get to know her just a little better before inviting her into"—Ripley craned her neck to see where Zoe and Nancy had gone—"Nancy's apartment?"

Chewing on my lip, I muttered, "Actually, she's going to rent the open apartment. She's just filling out the paperwork now."

"What?" Ripley's face went taut with anger. Her fingers curled into fists. "That was pretty fast, if you ask me. Not that anyone did, so—fine. It's fine."

"Fine."

"Great."

"Great."

"Come on, Addy," Ripley said, storming off.

Just as they moved to the other side of the lobby, Zoe emerged from Nancy's apartment.

"You're in?" I asked hopefully, since she hadn't been in there for very long.

"She's going to run my credit, but as long as that's good, I can move in tomorrow." Zoe was practically glowing.

"Yay!" I resisted the urge to jump up and down with excitement, knowing Ripley was nearby, probably already staring daggers at me. Then I worried that my fight with Ripley was showing on my face when I noticed Zoe's was scrunched into a frown. "Wait. That's a good thing, right?"

"Yes, it's good." She flinched. "I'm sorry. I have to come clean about something. I may have been using you, just a little." She held her thumb and index finger just centimeters apart.

Ripley shot me a scowl from across the lobby, and I didn't miss that she floated closer.

"What do you mean?" I really didn't want Ripley to be right after the disagreement we'd had.

"I really wanted to get into this building," Zoe admitted.

Ripley let out a low, "Told ya so…"

My heart sank. Ripley had been right. Zoe *had* been using me, just like Kirsten. Embarrassment at thinking we'd been friends swirled through me, destroying any confidence I'd accumulated through the situation.

"My dad used to live here," Zoe explained, "and I'm looking for information about him. Since Mom died, this is all I've got. That's why I sat down and talked to you at first. I wanted an *in* at the Morrisey. But then you and I hit it off, and I wanted to move in even more."

Wait. That wasn't like Kirsten at all. In fact, it was completely understandable. I was about to shoot an equally petty *told ya so* look back at Ripley when a soft hand landed on my shoulder. I jumped, not realizing anyone had been behind me.

"Iris," I let my neighbor's name out in a squeal as I

turned around. "Hi." I lunged toward her, enveloping her in a tight hug.

"Hey, kiddo. Good to see you." Her soft voice felt like a scarf wrapping around my shoulders.

She'd left Aunt Penny in Scotland last week, but she'd stopped to see her family for a few days in Iowa, so she'd only just got in, well, today, it seemed.

Iris Finley stood back. "Well?" she asked. "Do I look like a Scottish lass?"

A laugh bubbled out of me. "Aye, ye do," I told her in my best Scottish accent.

I'd practiced that accent a lot with Penny over the years. After dozens of best-selling historical Scottish romances, Penny had a pretty good accent herself, and we had fun practicing some of the tamer lines she wrote for her Scottish heroes. Iris, my Aunt Penny's best friend, in addition to being my neighbor in 5B, had just returned from a month-long visit to my aunt's new house in the Highlands.

She peered around me to get a better look at Zoe. "Hello."

"Oh, sorry." I stepped back so we were more of a circle. "Iris, this is Zoe. She's a new friend, and she's going to be renting 5E."

Iris took Zoe's outstretched hand, greeting her before eyeing me. "Five E?"

While Penny had filled her in on the murder in 3B and Opal Halifax moving into that unit, Iris had been traveling once I'd learned about Quentin asking Nancy to rent out the apartment.

"I'll fill you in later," I told her. "Zoe, here, works right around the corner, so this is—" I was about to talk about how convenient the location was for her, not wanting to spill the real reason she wanted to live in the Morrisey, but Zoe cut me off.

"I don't know who my dad is, like Meg here, and I'm hoping to learn more about him. All I know is that he used to live here." Zoe's calm expression showed me it was okay, that she didn't want to keep any more secrets. "I hoped moving in would get me closer to figuring out who he was."

Iris's eyes widened. "Oh, very nice. Okay." Her cheeks reddened a little, and she glanced nervously at me. "Well, let me know if you have questions. I didn't move in until the midnineties, but maybe I can be of help. For now, I'm going to unpack." She patted her large rolling suitcase.

Waving, we said goodbye as she rolled over to the elevator.

"That's our neighbor," I told her. "She's a research librarian at the Seattle Public Library. If anyone can help you with information about your dad, I'm sure she can. The group over there might also know something." I jerked my head toward the older residents over in the sitting area of the lobby.

"Right. Is it weird that I feel a little paralyzed now that I have a path forward?" Zoe laughed nervously. She turned to me. "Having your help makes the task seem less daunting. That is, if you'll help me."

"Of course I'll help you. We can start asking around tomorrow when you're moving in." I emphasized "when," assuming her background check and credit score would pass

Nancy's scrutiny. I ignored the snort of indignation that came from Ripley, who was full-on pouting.

"Thank you so much."

I wrinkled my nose. "Now it's my turn to tell you the truth."

Zoe's eyes flashed with interest.

"The man who used to live in the apartment you want to rent … killed another resident last week. That's why his place is available." I studied her. "And there was just a body found in the Underground between our building and your work, actually. I found it."

"Whoa, that *is* a lot. But don't worry," she said, when I cringed. "That kinda stuff doesn't bother me." Zoe checked her watch. "I need to head to work. Talk tomorrow?"

We exchanged numbers before she left. By the time I turned around, Ripley and Addy were gone. Heading upstairs by myself, I—possibly vindictively—decided to do some research on Paris Elliott.

I went to the Elliott Distillery website first, wondering if I might find anything to do with the feud. Unsurprisingly, there wasn't a thing about the Stimacs. But I found a list of the Elliott family members and their positions within the company. Foster Elliott was listed as the company's CEO. His smug picture gave me the chills, and his bio about the proud legacy of his family made me feel ill. The CFO had been the other man who'd come to the Morrisey that evening to threaten us. And Sophia, the blonde-haired woman, who'd referred to Paris as her sister, was listed as the head distiller for the company. The bio under her picture listed her interest in chemistry and biology and talked about how she loved experimenting with new botanicals. The page listed Paris as the head of marketing and social media accounts.

Checking said accounts, I found a ton of pictures of both Paris and the distillery's flagship gin, a recipe they'd been using for almost a hundred years. The idea of a mostly family-run business made me momentarily wonder about nepotism, and whether Paris had truly earned her place in the company. That could be a tempting motive for murder. But I quickly put those thoughts to rest as I scoured the pages.

Paris really had been good at her job, it seemed. The Elliott Distillery accounts were beautiful, curated images of the ingredients they used, pictures of their antique still, and constant shout-outs to the new partnerships she was creating in the industry.

I reread one post from last week that sounded more like a fact check. Paris, writing as Elliott Distillery, wanted to clear up any rumors that they were partnering with a company called Boutique Liquor. She mentioned they were not and would never work with a company with such a poor record of supporting their workers, adding that Elliott Distillery stood behind fair wages and working conditions for delivery drivers.

Pressing my lips forward, impressed by her commitment to fair business practices, I moved on to Paris's personal accounts, hoping to find more there. She was just as talented at curating her personal life as she was with the company account, if her number of followers and post likes were anything to go by.

In the sea of pictures of her posing in different outfits around the city, one stood out to me. It was Paris, standing on the other side of the window I'd stood at earlier with Ripley and Addy. The Emmie's logo was backward in Paris's picture. Addy had mentioned how much her family loved going there, and it seemed like the Elliotts hadn't ever gotten over their love of the diner. Maybe I would have to check it out. If the family had been eating there for over a century, the people who owned it might have information no one else did.

After that, I made myself something to eat, Anise curled in my lap, and I lost myself in research. I knew Ripley wouldn't understand, but I completely got Gavin's obsession with the century-old feud. I could feel myself getting sucked in, and I couldn't help but feel it in my bones that this was the key to solving more than one mystery.

Eleven

The next day, I helped Zoe move her stuff into apartment 5E. It turned out that our similarities didn't end with our parental history. We liked a lot of the same music, television, and she was incredibly easy to talk to.

Each time Zoe and I laughed together or found another thing in common, it only added to the smugness I felt about Ripley being oh-so-wrong about my new friend. She was definitely a Jasmine, not a Kirsten.

Zoe wanted all the details on the deaths I'd mentioned yesterday in the lobby. She'd heard about Paris's body, especially when the police had come in to question her bosses, Kaden and Blake Stimac, but I filled her in on the rest. Based on what the Stimacs said about the family in the wake of the police visiting, it didn't surprise her that Foster Elliott had called in favors to get me banned from the galleries I'd applied to. While we worked, I repeated a lot of what Gavin had told me the day before.

When we'd exhausted that topic, Zoe wanted to know about Mr. Miller's death in 3B. That conversation morphed into me showing her the passage in her wardrobe, telling her all about my crush on Laurie, his work trip to Japan, and even my indecision with my career.

"There aren't any openings at the speakeasy, are there?" I asked as we loaded the elevator with another round of her boxes. "I get you an apartment. You get me a job?" I sent Zoe a big, cheesy smile.

She shot me a glare that made me worry she'd turned into Ripley for a moment. "Meg, no. You don't want to work there. You need to work at a gallery or at least do something with your art."

I snorted. "Right. I want to, but that doesn't seem like it's going to work with the Elliotts thwarting me at every turn. The Stimacs might be the only people in the city who want to hire me. They seem to be the only ones who will go against what the Elliotts want."

But even as I said it, I wasn't sure I wanted to work for them. While the Stimacs had been suspects in Detective Anthony's eyes from the moment she learned Paris's last name, they'd definitely moved up in mine ever since we found that secret passage into their speakeasy. Neither Zoe nor I were Elliotts, though, so we were technically safe from the murderous family feud. Still, I was glad Ripley wasn't here to hear me ask about the possibility of me working for them. I hadn't seen her or Addy since the lobby yesterday.

Zoe clapped the dust from her hands and glanced around. "What do you say we take a break and have some lunch? My treat."

"That sounds great. What are you thinking?"

She shrugged. "You know this area better than me."

I did, but it wasn't just that. With my plan to go to Emmie's and find out information about the Elliotts, I'd never dreamed I'd have a friend to take with me. Having Zoe by my side calmed any jitters I was feeling about heading into a favorite haunt of a powerful family that had already proven they didn't like me and would hurt me if they could.

That solidified it. "There's a place I was thinking of trying out," I told Zoe.

She squinted one eye at me. "Then why do you look like you're about to get away with something?"

"Paris Elliott frequented the place," I admitted. "And ... I may or may not be looking into who murdered her."

Zoe rubbed her hands together. "Like you solved the case with Mr. Miller?"

"Hopefully." I smiled weakly.

Her eyes focused on something in the distance for a moment. "Can I help? I mean, I know Laurie was your partner in the last case, but since he's not here?"

My weak smile grew in strength. "I'd love to have help."

"Yes." She pumped her fist in the air. "This is so exciting. I'm in. Show me the way."

I couldn't help but laugh at her enthusiasm. We popped across the hallway to my apartment so I could grab my purse.

I checked on Zoe as we made our way down the stairs. "I don't mean to put Paris before helping you figure out who your dad is."

"I don't feel like that's what's happening," she assured

me. "We're just following a lead. Technically, we don't have any leads on my dad."

"Yet. We could chat with some of the other residents once we get back this evening."

Zoe wrinkled her nose. "I've got to work tonight."

"Oh, right." I glanced down at my shoes. "Well, soon, then. I haven't forgotten."

"I know. I trust you."

My chest felt warm. I trusted her too. Ripley was wrong. She had to be.

It was slightly after one when we made our way to Emmie's, and either we'd missed the big lunch rush, or the place really wasn't that popular. Following the host to a seat in the corner, it was easy enough to monitor the other customers, since there were only about a dozen people inside.

The smell of sizzling french fries wafted through the restaurant. Examining the menu, it seemed full of traditional lunch fare. The host brought us waters and told us our server would be with us soon. I thought about asking the host about Paris, but another group came in right after us, and he had to shuffle off to seat them. My questions would have to wait until our server arrived.

Less than a minute later, a woman in a black T-shirt came to take our orders. I ordered the turkey club, and Zoe opted for the tuna, but before the server could leave, I said, "We heard Paris Elliott used to frequent this restaurant. Is that true?"

The server checked over her shoulder. "She came here at least once a week."

"Did you notice anything suspicious that could've led to her death?" Zoe asked.

Previously polite, the server's expression turned icy as she regarded us like we were pests in her restaurant. "Look, it wasn't just Paris. All the Elliotts come here—a lot. I don't want to get caught talking about them."

I understood, having experienced the family when they were upset and knowing, firsthand, what power they wielded in the community. I should've guessed the place the family had been coming to for over a century would keep their allegiances clear.

The server left, and I turned to Zoe. "Well, it was worth a try. Let's eat and get out of here as soon as possible."

Zoe agreed. We turned to our drinks, as if we were on a timeline to get out of there now that there wasn't any information we could learn from the staff.

"So, is the Morrisey the only thing your mom told you about your dad?" I asked, trying to pass the time.

"Yeah," Zoe confirmed. "She just mentioned that she used to live in Seattle, and she met him when he lived in a funky old building in Pioneer Square. I eventually got the building name out of her, but she was really closed off about who he was and why she left him. She just said it got complicated, and she had to put me first."

My heart ached for Zoe, knowing the odd sense of loss she felt.

"That's a lot more than I know about mine. The only thing I know is that my mom didn't want him in my life. So, when she died, I went straight to my Aunt Penny instead of him." I waved a hand as if it were that easy to let go.

As Zoe studied me, obviously seeing through my dismissive gesture, our server arrived with our food, plopping the plates in front of us a little unceremoniously. I suppose we deserved that kind of treatment when we'd pried into the lives of some of their regulars. Zoe and I dug in.

"Do you think you'll ever look into who your dad is?" Zoe asked after a few bites, proving she knew my dad's identity wasn't as easy to brush off as I tried to pretend.

"I don't think I will. It seems like the one thing my mom wanted, so going against it makes me feel like I'm letting her down, you know?"

Zoe widened her eyes. "For sure. It took me a long time to decide to move because I knew my mom loved Vermont and talked about how happy she was to live there. But through my grief, I realized that what she needed and what I needed were two different things, and that's okay. I need family, and I thought finding my dad would be an easy way to accomplish that."

I liked her line of reasoning, and I didn't blame her for craving the idea of family once her mom was gone. As much as I'd felt the loss of my mom, I had Ripley, Aunt Penny, and my Morrisey family. While Zoe had gotten decades longer with her mom than I had, now that her mother was gone, it sounded like she was all alone. I wasn't sure which situation was worse.

As we talked, we kept an eye on the door, scanning everyone who entered, just in case the Elliotts stopped by for a late lunch. But as we got further into the topic of our fathers, I realized I'd stopped paying attention to the front door, or who was entering.

Just then, a server walked by with a gorgeous slice of pie. The peachy flavor of the pie wafted over to me so intensely, reminding me of the sickly-sweet peach flavor I'd smelled around Paris's body.

"Yum, peach pie," Zoe said, proving she had no such qualms about the smell of peaches. "I think I need a slice of that in my life." Her eyes followed the dessert, but mine were caught somewhere else.

Because a new party had entered the restaurant. And they were staring directly at me, coming toward me, actually. Anger seeped from Foster Elliott's bones as he stopped in front of me, hunched in irritation.

"I thought I told you to stay away from us?" His voice was tight, and he pointed to the door. "You need to leave, now."

Our server shuffled over, wide eyed, with our check in her hand. "I'm so sorry, Mr. Elliott. These two were just about to pay."

"Actually, we were considering dessert." Zoe lifted her chin in defiance.

Something dark passed behind Foster Elliott's eyes as his gaze snaked over Zoe. But before he could say anything, Sophia strode over, fiddling with her purse. "Dad, calm down. It's not a good look to kick people out of a restaurant." She eyed the other patrons, who were staring. "Paris would be the first one to remind you of that. Remember, *optics*." She touched his arm oh-so-gently, and the man relaxed.

Foster snarled out a smile. "Of course." Turning to the

server, he said, "Shannon, they're fine. We can coexist while they finish." He walked away, our server on his heels.

And then it was just Sophia standing in front of us.

"Thank you?" I didn't mean to phrase it as a question, but I was so surprised by her help that I wasn't sure what else to say.

Sophia snorted. "It wasn't for you. Believe me. I don't like you or the people from your building any more than he does. But I don't believe you killed my sister."

"Wait. Why?" Zoe asked.

Sophia glared at her. "Because I know who did."

Her sentence felt like a slap to the face. Zoe must've agreed because she sucked in a quick breath.

"Did you tell the police?" I asked.

Her lips parted. "The police? Oh, man. Why didn't I think of that?" The act fell at the end, and her expression flattened with annoyance. "Of course I told them. But if they don't care that my sister got in a huge fight with Blake Stimac the day before she was found dead, I can't do anything more to convince them."

"Blake?" Zoe's posture stiffened at the name.

And while Zoe was probably starting a mental list of reasons it couldn't have been her boss, I was privy to information she wasn't, specifically about the hidden passage between the Underground and the office of The Cooler.

Then, proving I wasn't the only one doing research on who everyone involved in this mystery was, Sophia leaned forward and told Zoe, "Better watch out. Looks like you're working for a murderer." And with that, she rejoined her family.

Zoe stared after them, mostly catatonic. Finally, she said, "How does she know who *I* am?"

"It's probably because you're hanging out with me. I'm sorry." I grimaced.

"No." Zoe dismissed my comment. "They probably know everything about anyone who works for the Stimacs. This isn't on you." Then, as if emboldened by the encounter, Zoe caught our server as she walked past. "Excuse me. I think we would like to add dessert, if that's okay."

Shannon checked over her shoulder at the Elliotts, but said, "Sure, what can I get you?"

"Can we have a slice of that peach pie that went by earlier?" Zoe elbowed me, having mistaken my reaction to the smell as interest.

Shannon paused. "We only have apple."

Odd. I could've sworn I smelled peach.

"Oh, that's okay. Right, Meg?" Zoe turned to me.

I nodded, in a bit of a daze.

As we waited for our pie, Zoe rubbed her hands together. "I know that run-in with the Elliotts was uncomfortable, but it was also the biggest clue you've gotten in the case, so far, right?" When I confirmed it was, she added, "I'm definitely going to do some digging tonight when I work. I have to know if it's Blake or not. I can't be working for a murderer."

Twelve

Almost immediately, I wished we hadn't stayed for pie. While the restaurant hadn't been crowded before, the addition of the Elliott family made it feel positively stifling, partly because they doubled the occupancy, and partly because they glared at us from across the room.

But I was more worried about what Zoe had just said. I turned in my seat. "Are you sure? Spying on your bosses sounds incredibly dangerous."

Zoe chewed on her lip. "So does working for a murderer."

She was right, and she also had a vested interest in figuring out if the Stimacs were the ones who'd hurt Paris, not to mention access to the family.

"You're the expert on this stuff. What should I ask Blake to figure out whether what Sophia said is true or not?" She elbowed me in the side.

I rolled my eyes. "I helped solve *one* case, and mostly I just stumbled onto the truth."

As easy as Zoe was to talk to, I couldn't share that the reason I'd gotten involved in that case was because the ghosts I talked to knew things the police didn't.

Our pieces of pie came, and we dug in. But as Zoe peppered me with more questions in between bites, I realized she wasn't going to buy the whole "I stumbled on to the truth" excuse. Given that I couldn't tell her about my ghosts, the only other explanation for me getting involved in multiple cases was if I was really into solving mysteries. It wasn't as if it was incorrect. I did like putting clues together, and I'd already proven that I had a hard time letting go when I learned information about a case.

I pointed my fork at Zoe between bites. "Well, first you have to find an inconspicuous way to figure out what he was doing on Sunday when Paris was killed. It can't sound like a line of questioning. You want it to be casual. Do you chat about your lives at work?"

"Sure. Kaden, the older one, keeps to himself more, but Blake is really fun to talk to." She cringed. "Which is part of what makes this so tough. He's been so nice to me in the past. But I can ask him what he was up to last weekend, easy."

"Try to make it seem like you were just gabbing about yourself and *your* weekend and that you've been taught manners and that you need to ask him about himself to balance out everything you've just said." I shrugged. That was actually pretty good advice.

Zoe nodded, popping the last bit of dessert into her mouth. "I can do that."

"And above all, be careful."

Even though she said she would, worry sat in my stomach alongside the apples in the pie, turning them sour.

※

That afternoon, Zoe went to get ready for her shift, and I went home. Ripley and Addy were inside, giving me a flip-flopping feeling of excitement to see them and then dread when I remembered how tense things were with me and Ripley at the moment.

"Hey," I said, plopping my purse down on the small table I kept right next to the front door.

"Hey," Ripley said.

Addy glanced between the two of us in discomfort.

"I see Zoe's moved in," Ripley scoffed.

I dipped my chin. A sassy retort about her spying on my new friend came to mind at first, but I swallowed it and said, "Mostly. She had to head to work. We got a tip that one of her bosses, Blake, got in a fight with Paris the day before she died, so she's going to do a little digging while she's there." Reminding myself that Zoe might text with an update at any moment, I pulled out my phone and took it with me as I plopped onto the couch.

Anise snuggled on the back, sleeping in a beam of sunlight. I thought about pulling her into my lap, but figured I'd let her sleep since she seemed to be comfortable.

"A Stimac, just like Detective Anthony thought," Ripley said.

"Did the two of you make any headway on Addy's case?"

They hadn't said they were going to keep looking into the colder of the two cases, but I knew my best friend. Even if she'd tried to convince me the gambling shootout had been the cause, she would make sure for Addy's sake.

"No." Addy wrung her hands in front of her.

Based on the multiple worried glances Addy directed at Ripley in the following seconds, added to the angry creases on Ripley's forehead, it was clear my best friend had fallen back into her depression about Clark. I winced. We'd just gotten her out of it, and then I'd gone and fought with her, pushing her right back into her sadness.

"Did the Squares have any information?" I asked, my question holding none of my earlier tightness. I hoped it sounded like a peace offering.

The Squares was the name Ripley and I used to describe the coterie of spirits who hung around Pioneer Square, especially the park outside our building where the famous pergola and totem pole stood. Collectively, they spanned the last two centuries.

Ripley tilted her head. She took my offering and said, "Victor is going to ask around about it, but he said Prohibition was a bit of a blur for him."

My phone buzzed with a text from Zoe.

> Blake and I chatted while we did our prep work before opening. He wouldn't tell me what he was doing last Sunday, and he got a little cagey about it when I pressed him.

I swore under my breath. As much as finding Paris's actual killer would help me get the Elliotts off my back and out of the way of getting a job, I was really hoping Blake wasn't the killer. Zoe not only loved her job, but she needed the money, especially now that she was renting 5E.

There was also the added, and terrifying, reality that it would mean she was working for a murderer.

"What? Why does your face look all pinched like that?" Ripley normally would've just read the text right over my shoulder. The fact that she didn't proved how uncomfortable things had gotten between us.

Mad at Ripley as I was, I couldn't let my pride stand in the way of Zoe's safety.

"It's Zoe. She asked Blake about Sunday and he didn't have an alibi. Not only that, but he got irritated the more she asked him about it." Worry crinkled my forehead as I glanced up at my friend.

I felt helpless and had to admit that solving a mystery without my usual ghostly help was a lot harder than I'd expected.

"We can go check on her," Ripley said, stepping forward.

Love for my best friend swelled in my heart. Even through our fight, she was there for me when I needed her.

"That would be great. But do you think you could split up?" I asked.

Despite everything I'd learned about Paris's murder over the past day, I was still missing one crucial piece of information: what had killed her.

Ripley nodded but cocked her head in question.

"Addy, would you go down to The Cooler? Make sure Zoe's okay? Rip, would you pay Detective Anthony a visit and see if you can figure out what was in that syringe that killed Paris before you join Addy?"

The ghosts agreed and disappeared. I paced in the apartment for the next few minutes. After a while, however, pacing wasn't enough. Sitting at my desk, I put aside the painting I'd been working on and pulled out a new canvas. Ever since I'd had that drink at The Cooler, with its black-and-white photos, I couldn't get the image of flappers out of my mind. Added to all the talk we'd been doing about the twenties, I felt a pull to paint something from that era.

Starting with the main subject, I sketched the outline of a flapper in the center of the piece before I moved to paint. Without strictly meaning to, I painted big doe eyes, brown hair, and bright red lips. Before long, Addy stared back at me from the canvas. It still seemed to be missing something, though.

Anise chose that moment to get up from her nap, stretch, and rub against my leg.

"Ani, you're right," I told the cat, thinking of the way she'd been particularly enthralled with Addy and her sparkly dress.

Dipping my brush in black, I added a little Anise look-alike to Addy's portrait. The cat balanced on the flapper's shoulders. It was whimsical and fun. I was just adding some Art Deco components in the background when Ripley returned, announcing herself as she usually did.

"Sorry that took so long." She puffed out her cheeks. "You know Detective Anthony. The woman holds things close to her chest, even within the office."

I wondered if that meant that Ripley had come up empty-handed.

"Oh! That's gorgeous, Megs." She nodded at the painting in front of me.

Dipping my head in thanks, I asked, "So you couldn't get any information about the murder weapon?"

Ripley's mouth cut into a scheming smile. "I didn't say *that*, did I? Apparently, Paris died of a nicotine overdose. She had a vape pen on her, and a bunch of the sticky liquid spilled on her dress when they found her body, but the amount in her system was so high that they ruled it wouldn't be possible from vaping alone."

"I haven't ever heard of someone dying from nicotine."

"Most of the officers hadn't either," Ripley explained. "Amaya was doing some research on it toward the tail end of her shift today."

Rocking back in my chair as I took in that news, I thought through the implications of the murder weapon. "Okay, can you go check on Addy and Zoe? I guess now that we know about the vaping, we need to check if Blake or any of his family members vape. That'll be our first step."

Ripley gave me a salute before she vanished.

I channeled the rest of my nervous energy into finishing

my painting as I waited. About halfway through the evening, I thought about going down to The Cooler and hanging out as a patron, but I didn't have unlimited money, especially since the Elliotts were blocking my ability to get a job at the moment, and I also didn't have a reservation. Zoe had made an exception because it had been early enough in the evening that it was slow, but I'd bet the place was packed at that time of night. So, I started a second painting. This time I made the flapper blonde, like Paris, choosing a different background design and adding a tabby cat cradled in her arms. Flappers and Felines, I could call the collection. The combination made me smile.

It was a testament to how much art was a positive influence in my life that I had a place to channel all the emotions I was feeling.

I was almost done with the second painting when Addy and Ripley showed up in the apartment. Looking down at my phone to see the time, I realized I'd missed another text from Zoe a few minutes ago.

> Hey, just off now. Going to head home and get some rest. I'm beat. Talk in the morning?

I responded with a thumbs-up, then turned my attention to the two ghosts who looked as ragged as Zoe's text sounded.

"How'd it go?"

"Well, there was nothing for a long time, but then..." Ripley shot a knowing look at Addy.

"Then Blake and his older brother, Kaden, disappeared

into the back office once Zoe left. They talked about her." Addy swallowed forebodingly.

"They mentioned that she's been asking around about Paris's death and that she pushed Blake on his alibi. They're worried about her. Kaden said he'd have people look into her, and Blake said he might need to take care of her." Ripley's expression dropped, like she regretted everything she'd ever said about the young woman.

"*Ugh.* That's worse than I thought. There's no way she can keep looking into this case now."

"Rejoin forces?" Ripley asked.

"Are you sure you're okay with Zoe?" I countered.

Ripley's lips twitched downward. "It's possible you were right about her being a Jasmine. Clark moving on made me ... wonder if I'll ever be at peace like that. I took it out on you, and I was unfairly critical of Zoe. You were right."

I swallowed hard. Ripley's pause during her statement about Clark moving on had glossed over a lot of things she wouldn't say. She didn't want me to blame myself for the fact that she was stuck here with me. But that was the reason she hadn't moved on. It was hard not to feel responsible for her unhappiness when she fell into these depressive states.

"You had your reasons," I croaked out, glad we were talking, but unsure of how to help her.

"Oh, thank goodness." Addy's shoulders slumped forward in relief. "You two were making me so nervous with how mad you were at each other." Suddenly, her attention caught on the paintings. She raced forward. "Is this me?"

Pride expanded through my chest as I confirmed it was.

"It's gorgeous, Megs." If Addy could've blushed, she

would've as she gave us both a sheepish smile. "I mean, I'm not saying *I'm* gorgeous, but you—"

"You are," Ripley and I said at the same time.

"Well, if you insist." Addy swatted in mock shyness at us.

We laughed, and it felt good to be back with my best friend. But as happy as I was about our reconciliation, that didn't change the fact that Zoe was in danger. Without telling her about my ability to talk to ghosts, I wasn't sure how I was going to get her to leave this case alone.

Thirteen

Ripley rubbed her hands together. "Okay, so now that we're on the same team again, I think we need to go through all the clues."

It was late, but my mind was abuzz with ideas, and it wasn't like I had a job I needed to get up for in the morning.

"Definitely." I put my art supplies away so I could get out a pad of paper.

Once I was ready, I plopped onto the couch and jotted down what we knew, narrating as I did so.

"Okay, so Paris Elliott was twenty-nine when she died."

My ghostly companions nodded along as I wrote.

"She was, for all intents and purposes, an influencer, right?" Ripley asked, showing she knew more about the case than I'd thought. She must've looked into it a little on her own as well.

Addy wrinkled her nose. "What's an influencer?"

"It's where they use social media to sell products. It's

new. Wasn't even a thing when I was alive." Ripley pointed to my paper.

Addy chewed on her lip as she listened, but I didn't stop to explain about social media, knowing she would ask if she was lost.

Tapping the notepad, I said, "Technically, but her official job title was head of marketing and social media accounts. From what I could see on the Elliott Distillery sites and Paris's personal social media account—"

But my sentence was cut short by my phone ringing with that same telltale video-call alert. It was late enough that it could've been Aunt Penny starting her morning. Ripley floated by where my phone sat on the desk, and her face peeled into the biggest grin.

"Uh, Addy and I will give you a little privacy for this one." She winked and ushered Addy out of the apartment in front of her.

Laurie.

My heartbeat shot through the roof with excitement. Biting my lip so I wouldn't be smiling so big when I answered his call, I rushed over to the desk to pick up my phone. Bringing it back to the couch, I did my usual mental math. It was very early in the morning in Japan.

Is he calling me before he goes to work? The thought made happiness flit through my entire body, ruining any attempt I'd made to not look like I was completely entranced with him as I answered the call.

Laurie's handsome face was furrowed with worry as it filled my screen. The background was the same, telling me he was in his hotel room again.

Once his eyes moved up and down the screen, he relaxed. "Oh, good. I didn't wake you, did I?" His forehead returned to the scrunched version from a moment ago for a split second as he waited for my answer.

"Nope. You know me. Night owl." I pointed to my chest.

He chuckled. "Penny taught you well."

I tilted my head. "Hey, I thought I was supposed to be the one to call you next."

"You were." He widened his eyes. "But it's been days since we talked, and I'm tired of waiting for you to call."

My heart melted. He'd been waiting for me? I guess the last few days had been pretty busy.

"I'm sorry." I ran a hand over my face. "I was helping a friend move into the open apartment on my floor, so I think I lost track of time."

"A *friend*?" Laurie asked. It wasn't in a way that made him sound surprised that I had a friend—which, given my track record, would've been fair. It was more in a teasing way that held a hint of digging, like he was wondering who this friend was. Or, whether the friend was a man or a woman.

Smiling at the realization that Laurie might be a little jealous, I said, "The bartender friend I was telling you about. The one who works at The Cooler. She was looking for a place, and I told her about the opening we had in the building."

Laurie bobbed his head in understanding. "That's perfect. How cool that you'll have a friend on your floor. Well, another one." I expected him to mention Iris, knowing she was like an aunt to me, but he said, "I know how close you and Edna are."

Amusement rippled through me. Edna Feldner had to be over a hundred years old. And even though she was as sweet as could be, it was hard to have a conversation with the woman because of her inability to hear very well and her constantly hunched-over stature. I always felt like I needed to kneel to talk to her, and then it seemed condescending, like I was treating her the same as I might a toddler.

"You know me and Edna," I said through another giggle.

Laurie's deep laugh felt like biting into the best, richest bite of crème brûlée, and I wanted to savor it forever.

"So, tell me, how's the case been going? Was Gavin able to help?" Laurie asked.

I blinked at the sudden change, trying to remind myself of what he knew and what had happened since we last talked.

"Gavin was an immense help," I said. "He's super knowledgeable about the feud between these two families."

It wasn't until I saw the smirk taking over Laurie's face that I realized I'd given myself away. Laurie had told me to give Gavin's number to Detective Anthony. He'd warned Gavin that the police might come to talk to him. But I'd used him for my research instead. From the way Laurie was looking at me, he'd expected no less.

Scratching at the side of my neck, I admitted, "Okay, you caught me. Yes, I talked to him first. I promise that I'll still let the police know that he's here to help, but it's all too interesting to pass up. Laurie, you wouldn't believe this stuff. These two families hate each other so much."

When he chuckled and told me it was okay, I told him the history I'd learned from Gavin, filling in where I could with information from Addy.

"But he didn't know who the skeleton could've belonged to?" Laurie asked.

I shook my head. "No more than the police do."

"Still, I think he might help them ... if Amaya will let him consult." His lips tugged to one side.

Had Laurie just alluded to the fact that Detective Anthony was a little stuck in her ways? I inwardly celebrated. His use of her first name didn't even bother me that time.

"She's also got her hands full with the more recent death," I said. "That one's concerning me a lot more too."

"Why's that?" Laurie's forehead furrowed.

I sniffed. "My new friend, Zoe, she works with the Stimacs at that speakeasy. Right now, I think they're the primary suspects in Paris's murder. I'm worried about her safety. She helped me do a little digging into the case, and the Stimacs somehow found out, so they're looking into her now."

Laurie's eyes went wide. "Really? How'd you find that out?"

I scolded myself for getting too comfortable and revealing something I knew only because of my ghostly contacts. How would I know that if my ghosts hadn't spied on the Stimacs?

"Uh, they flat out told her. Warned her to her face." I pressed my lips forward, willing him to believe the lie.

"Bold," Laurie said.

Phew.

"Right? I'll make sure she stays out of things from now on, though," I told him, seeing worry tinge his features.

"Good." He turned his head and shot me a sidelong glance. "And you make sure you're staying safe too, okay?"

I told him I would, then added, "Tell me all about Japan. How are things going?"

A smile cut across his face. "It's amazing. It's such a beautiful place and the people are so nice." He let out a deep chuckle. "I've eaten a few things that I have no idea what they are, but everything's been delicious. Oh, I took a trip to see this amazing Buddha statue yesterday…"

I settled my head on the couch as I listened.

I WOKE WITH A START.

After hanging up with Laurie, I'd looked up a few of the places he'd mentioned, wanting to see pictures of where he'd visited. I must've literally fallen asleep on my phone last night, because it buzzed against my right cheek and was slightly wet from drool.

It buzzed again.

Checking the screen and seeing that it was already nine in the morning, I expected it to be Zoe, sending me text after text, wondering when I wanted to debrief about what she'd learned yesterday, unaware that I already knew way more than she did about the situation at the speakeasy.

But it wasn't Zoe at all. It was Gavin Cross, and it wasn't a constant barrage of texts. He was calling me.

"Gavin, hey," I said in the least-groggy voice I could muster. I think I still sounded like I'd just woken up, though.

That was confirmed when Gavin said, "Meg. Hey, sorry to call so early."

Gavin didn't seem like the kind of person who thought

of nine in the morning as early, so he was most likely just being nice.

"No worries. What's up?" I sat up, noting that Ani was over by her food bowl, eating a little morning snack, so I wasn't in danger of disturbing her as I kicked my legs off the couch.

"Well..." He cleared his throat. "I have a proposition for you."

"Okay." I hoped I did a better job of concealing my apprehension than I had with my grogginess.

"There's an event coming up tonight, and I was wondering if you wanted to be my plus-one." Between the way he spat out the sentence as if he might chicken out if he hesitated, and the slight shake to his voice, I could tell he was nervous.

Closing my eyes tight, I pulled in a breath through my nose to steady my suddenly frenetic heartbeat. Was Laurie's friend about to ask me out?

It was like Gavin could hear the frantic thoughts rushing through my mind, though, because he added, "Platonically, of course."

"Oh." I was too stunned to say anything more.

"From the way Laurence described you back in college, I'd say he's kind of into you, so I don't want to step on his toes at all. I thought you might be interested in coming to the event for research."

Gavin's words swam around me in a happy explosion of fireworks. Laurie had sounded like he was into me? Back in college?

Coming out of the happy fog, I latched on to the last

thing he'd said. "Wait. What research?"

"It's the hundredth anniversary of the Elliott family distillery this year, and they're doing a rebrand of their flagship gin," he explained. "They're having a big, Prohibition-style party, and the historical society got an invitation. I know you said you were interested in learning more about the feud. This is a perfect chance to see the Elliotts in all their glory. Sorry, this is so last-minute. My coworker who was supposed to attend is sick, so I'm the alternate."

I blinked. "Gavin, that sounds ... amazing. Yes, I'd love to go with you. Thank you for thinking of me."

He exhaled so loudly, I could tell he'd been holding it in. "Oh, great. Perfect." He told me where to meet him and explained that the dress code was nineteen twenties' costumes. "They're really playing up the Prohibition angle. The invitation called it a bootlegger ball."

"Got it." I had just the ghost to help me with a flapper outfit.

After I hung up with Gavin, I got myself ready, drank some coffee to fully wake up, and headed up to my favorite thrift store by Pike Place Market. I texted with Zoe while I walked.

> How was the rest of work last night?

Zoe must've been up by then because she texted back immediately.

> Fine. We were super busy so I didn't get a chance to talk any more to Blake or Kaden about anything other than bar stuff.

I gritted my teeth. But what she'd asked Blake during their prep had been enough to increase his suspicion surrounding her. Knowing my own hatred for whenever Ripley told me what to do, I tread carefully as I sent my next message.

> Are you worried about working there still? Are they creeping you out?

> To be honest? A little. But they're both off tonight, so my shift today will be fine. Maybe we can talk tomorrow and plan what to do next.

The worry perched on my shoulders lessened slightly at that news. At least she was safe tonight.

> Definitely. I got invited to a party tonight, but I'll be around tomorrow.

I tucked my phone into my purse as I reached the thrift store. There was a handful of dresses I would've chosen for a flapper costume prior to meeting Addy. But after spending time with her this week, a simpler beaded dress caught my eye first. It was a little big on me, but I figured that was also part of the style. I found some gloves and picked out a few pieces of costume jewelry from the accessories section before calling it good.

Addy and Ripley were back at the apartment once I

returned from the thrift store. Holding up my bags, I looked at Addy specifically.

"Any chance you can help make me into a flapper girl?"

She squealed and clapped her hands together.

By the time we were an hour out from the party, I looked like Addy's twin. My dress was brighter and more modern than hers, but I figured it was close enough. My hair, however, that was a hundred percent accurate. Addy made sure of it.

Addy also showed me a few dance moves and told me some fun twenties' phrases to use. Ripley interrupted our laughter.

"Okay, now that you know how to be the perfect party girl, we need to talk about the Elliotts and how you're going to handle them. This is a party they're throwing, after all, and you're not exactly their favorite." Ripley eyed me.

I gulped. "Right. A plan. That's a good idea." Sitting on the couch, we started talking strategy.

Fourteen

Elliott Distillery's Centennial Gin party took up the street floor of an event space near Occidental Park, just around the corner from the gallery I'd applied to the other day. Over the years, I'd seen wedding receptions, art shows, and even a bar mitzvah take place there. A bootlegger ball was a first.

I tried not to stare longingly at the funky art gallery I'd loved as I passed by on my way to the party, but Ripley must've noticed because she nodded in encouragement as I stalled. Right. Helping figure out who actually killed Paris was a great way to get the Elliotts to rescind the favors they must've called in around the community. Maybe if they didn't hate me anymore, I'd have a second shot at that gallery.

After having Addy fuss with my outfit, I saw the twenties' costumes the other women wore in a different light. They were all far too gaudy, and their hair was all wrong. I checked my judgments, though, knowing they didn't have an authentic flapper to guide them like I did.

The sun was just beginning to set, blanketing the event in a gorgeous peach-colored light. Less natural light allowed the thousands of twinkling lights that had been strung through the venue to truly shine. Twenties' music, heavy on the brass instruments and novelty piano, filled the room.

Addy hummed in appreciation as she twisted her legs, kicked her feet out, and splayed her hands in arcs in a smaller version of the Charleston. I watched her out of the corner of my eye, counting off the steps like she'd taught me earlier. I still wasn't feeling particularly confident about the idea of performing the dance myself. Ripley cackled as she tried, doing a fairly good job for a girl whose idea of dancing had been head banging to her favorite grunge bands. But her chunky black boots made her look slow and clumsy compared to Addy's delicate flats.

Gavin stood just inside the venue, waiting for me. He looked nice. Between his dark hair, which he'd slicked back, and the suspenders he wore, he was most likely accurately dressed for the period. Like me, he didn't look as flashy as a lot of the other partygoers, who looked more like they'd been plucked from the set of *The Great Gatsby* movie. Gavin's commitment to accuracy didn't surprise me. The man was a historian. He was more likely to get the costume right than anyone else here—well, other than Addy.

Speaking of Addy, she nodded in approval as she took him in, something Gavin repeated as he looked me up and down.

"Very nice, Meg." He bobbed his head in appreciation as he stepped closer. "I'm impressed."

Curtsying, as Addy taught me, I said, "Thanks for inviting me."

My anxiety surrounding what might happen if—or when—I ran into one of the Elliotts dropped to the pit of my stomach as I looked around. But the costumes seemed to do their job. I couldn't immediately pick out any of the Elliotts, even though I'd seen them multiple times.

I had to hope the same would be true about my costume.

Ripley and Addy wandered through the party, careful to avoid people, but I could see their spirits shimmer as a few partygoers surprised them by changing direction and walking straight through them. While Ripley's jaw tightened each time it happened, Addy seemed unaffected, far too happy to be "back in the twenties" to be bothered by anything tonight.

"Shall we grab drinks?" Gavin gestured over to the large ornate bar set up near the back wall.

I followed behind, eyes poring over the menu of a handful of Prohibition-style cocktails that featured gin. Smiling, I ordered a French 75, while Gavin asked for a Gin Rickey. He tipped the bartender, and we wandered away with our drinks.

"So, Laurie said you two met in college?" I asked once we found a small standing table to perch near in the corner. It was a feat of epic proportions that I'd asked that question instead of asking Gavin to repeat everything that had caused him to believe Laurie was into me, like I wanted to.

Gavin sipped on his drink, eyeing it appreciatively before answering my question. "They randomly paired us as roommates during freshman year. We've stayed in touch ever since. He's a great guy."

"He really is." I sipped my cocktail.

The lemon peel and rosemary garnish hit my nose first. My thoughts returned to what Addy had divulged about the rosemary smell in the Morrisey's lobby, and I inwardly chuckled at the knowledge. Sipping the drink, I almost giggled at the bright, bubbly cocktail. It still wasn't quite as good as the one Zoe had made me the other night, but it was a close second. The Elliotts might not be my favorite family—besides Addy, of course—but they sure knew how to make gin.

"Sorry," Gavin said, tugging at his tie. He pulled out a vape pen and wiggled it in the air. "I'm going to get a little fresh air. I'll be right back."

Left alone, I took the opportunity to check out the venue. Along one wall, the botanicals for their Centennial Gin were listed like a recipe written out in chalk, though they didn't divulge how much of each was used or anything else about the process. It was fascinating to see. Not being a frequent gin drinker, I hadn't realized so many things went into the complex taste. Fennel, coriander, and rosemary were just a few of the ingredients.

Moving on from the botanicals, I studied the people a little closer and finally located the Elliotts. Foster looked even more intimidating in his twenties' getup, his outfit making him seem like an old-timey mobster who could order a guy with a silly nickname to see to it that I was "sleeping with the fishes" by morning.

Sophia's blonde hair was pinned back in an elegant updo that I think Addy would've approved of. Her black dress looked so similar to Addy's that I would've guessed it had been passed down as a family heirloom if I hadn't seen the remains of it clinging to Addy's skeleton in the Underground. In fact, dressed up the way she was, Sophia almost looked exactly like the second twenties' girl I'd painted last night.

Gavin returned while I was people-watching. He must've caught my attention on the host family because he said, "I need to go over and pay my respects to the hosts. Want to come with me?"

Fear and embarrassment crawled up my neck. "Uh, I think I'll stay here. You go." I flicked my fingers toward him.

If Gavin had questions about why I didn't want to be around the Elliotts, he didn't voice them. He simply raised his drink to me and wandered over to the family. A few moments later, he'd ducked his head in conversation with Foster Elliott.

Heartbeat ratcheting up, I wondered if I should've warned Gavin that I wasn't Elliott's favorite. Would Foster ask Gavin about his date? While I'd noticed them, it seemed the excitement of the party had given me enough of an invisibility cloak, and they either hadn't noticed me yet, or they weren't going to let my presence ruin their party.

Whatever Gavin was saying to Foster seemed to surprise the host, and not in a good way. His chin jutted back. I wasn't a lip reader, but I could clearly see that Foster was upset, as he glanced up, eyes searching the crowd. I froze, my breath caught in my lungs. But instead of settling on me, the elder Elliott found his daughter in the throng. He called Sophia over, and she joined their discussion.

My pulse settled as Gavin shook hands with the two of

them a few moments later, returning to my side.

"Everything okay?" I asked warily.

Gavin winked. "It is now."

I didn't know what that meant, but he didn't elaborate. My nerves were still too frayed from watching the interaction that I didn't push him. If it had anything to do with me, I would've known by now. I hoped.

As the evening wore on, I quickly realized the history of Pioneer Square wasn't the only thing Gavin was an expert on. The man knew just about everyone in attendance, and he had little tidbits about each of them. Many of the tidbits were things like, "Margaret owns that new macaron shop a block over." Others were juicier, like, "Greg, who bought the café down the street with his partner, just left her for the competitor a few blocks down."

But if I'd thought that gossip was big, it was nothing compared to when Blake and Kaden Stimac stepped inside. The brothers had gone all out with their costumes; they were decked out in what looked like authentic nineteen twenties' suits, complete with suspenders and spats. Like Gavin, their authenticity stuck out among a sea of costumes.

So, that was why they weren't working with Zoe tonight.

"Whoa. I can't believe the Elliotts invited the Stimacs," I whispered to Gavin as he stared at the newcomers, just like me and everyone else in the room.

Gavin kept his eyes on the brothers. "Technically, they're always invited to Elliott gatherings. Foster makes sure everyone knows that. But this is the first time in a while I've seen them show. It usually means there's extra drama between the families."

Foster raised his glass toward the Stimac brothers and sent them a smile so large it looked positively wicked. But there was one Elliott who seemed unable to keep her emotions in check in the presence of the rival family.

Sophia charged over to the Stimacs, glaring. "You have a lot of nerve coming here after what you did to Paris." She jabbed her index finger into Blake's chest, shoving back her shoulders so she stood at her full height, even though it still left her at least half a foot shorter than both Blake and Kaden.

Blake looked like he was about to say something to Sophia, but his brother stepped in front of Sophia instead, placing a palm on Blake's chest and pushing him back.

"We're not like *you* people." Kaden's dark eyes locked on to Sophia.

"What's that supposed to mean?" She bit out the question.

He barked out a curt laugh and pointed at the wall where the ingredients for their Centennial Gin were posted. "This isn't even your recipe. You stole it from my family. And now you're out here flaunting it like you somehow came up with it on your own."

"If we stole the recipe, your family stole that building out from under us." Sophia sniffed.

They stared each other down for a few more tense seconds before Sophia huffed, turned on her heel, and stomped over to the bar. The sound of a microphone clicked on, and Sophia stepped in front of the bar. People moved back, making room for her to speak. At first I thought she was going to use the "stage" as a way to publicly shame the

Stimacs. Instead, she launched into what seemed like a practiced speech.

"Thank you all for coming," she said, scanning the room. "We're so excited to share our family legacy with you. I'm so proud of what my family has accomplished so far in one hundred years with this gin, and I can't wait to see where the future takes us. For the next year, at least, there are some exciting things happening. I won't say *big*, but they're new directions for us here at Elliott Distillery." Turning off the mic, Sophia bowed slightly and returned to the bar.

"How's that for firsthand feud experience?" Gavin whispered out of the corner of his mouth, shooting his eyebrows up as he finally tore his gaze from Sophia to look at me. But something else caught his attention. "And the surprises keep coming."

"What?" I followed where he was looking, trying not to be too obvious.

Gavin jerked his head toward where Sophia had retreated after her speech. "That man Sophia's talking to at the bar is Ryan Dee, the owner of Boutique Liquor. I'm surprised they showed."

That name rang a bell. "Paris posted about them." I snapped my fingers. "She said they wouldn't ever be caught working with them." My eyes pored over the way Sophia and Ryan were smiling and then shaking hands. "Sure looks like that's not the case."

"It wouldn't surprise me if that was a decision Paris made without her family's input." A muscle tightened in Gavin's jaw. "That seemed to happen a lot."

I narrowed my eyes at Ryan. "What did Paris mean in her post about the way Boutique Liquor treats their employees?"

Gavin's eyes widened in recognition. "Oh. A few years ago, Boutique Liquor settled some lawsuits about the working conditions they were putting their delivery drivers through. From what I heard, Ryan made things better in the sense that he can't get sued anymore, but he doesn't do much more than the bare minimum." Gavin shook his head. "Regardless, I'm sure he wishes everyone would forget about that. He rebranded and everything. The company used to be called Liquor Direct. I'm surprised he isn't livid with Elliott Distillery for reminding everyone that they're one and the same."

Or possibly he knew it was Paris and blamed her, I thought to myself. Could Ryan Dee be yet another suspect in Paris's murder?

"But from what Sophia said about new directions, and how she went to talk to Ryan right after the speech, I'd bet anything they're partnership is back on." Gavin lifted his brows with interest.

Just as I was about to suggest that we go over and talk to Ryan to see if he had an alibi for the Sunday when Paris was killed, Foster Elliott spotted me.

"Uh, Meg, do you know Foster?" Gavin asked, his tone lilting up in question.

I wrinkled my nose as I realized I definitely should've filled him in on my history with the family before accepting his invitation. Foster took a few steps toward me, his progress halted by someone holding out a hand to congratulate him on the party.

"I do," I said carefully, then blurted out as quick of an explanation as I could to summarize our interactions. "He and I may or may not have gotten into a yelling match at the Morrisey after Paris died." I looked up at Gavin in apology.

But when I met Gavin's eyes, I didn't see understanding or even intrigue like I expected. Instead, the kind, gossipy man I'd spent the evening with so far was gone. In his place, a furious version stared down at me.

"You can't be serious," he scoffed as he raked his fingers through his hair. "This can't ... I can't ... not after everything. How could you let me bring you here knowing that?" Gavin gripped the back of his neck as if to ground himself. "You need to leave. Before he comes over here and sees me with you. Now." His dark eyes bore into me, leaving absolutely no room for doubt that he was serious.

Heart hammering with adrenaline and hurt, I paused for only a moment to say, "Gavin, I'm so sorry," before I abandoned the rest of my French 75 and ran toward the door.

I couldn't see where Ripley or Addy were, but I didn't have time to gather them. This place wasn't far enough from the Morrisey that Ripley would be pulled after me, so maybe they'd be able to stay and keep an eye on what was going on.

My run turned into a walk as the sounds of the party faded into the background. Tears stung my eyes as I tried to process what had happened. Sure, I'd been wrong not to tell him, but I hadn't expected that intense of a reaction.

Smug as I'd been at the party about how authentic my costume had turned out, I felt decidedly less excited about the beaded dress and my twenties' hairdo as I walked through Occidental Park and back to the Morrisey. My comfort zone when it came to living in a big city was all about not standing out. Tonight, people stared and whispered at the girl in the flapper dress with tears streaming down her face.

So by the time I reached the sanctuary of my building, I emptied my lungs in relief and dried my eyes. Darius, Art, and Opal simply nodded in my direction and let me pass by without comment. Either I'd done a good enough job getting rid of the evidence of my crying, or they could tell I needed to be alone. I even surprised myself by choosing the elevator rather than the stairs, feeling the weight of the evening settle over me.

Once the doors closed behind me, and I waited for the thing to move, I toed out of my black flats and ignored all the parts of the elevator that made me nervous. But as I stepped out into the fifth-floor hallway, I had a whole new set of worries.

Zoe paced in between our apartments, the door to her place open. Just the thought of being able to debrief what had happened with my friend already felt like a weight off my shoulders.

"Hey—" I started, but didn't get further than that.

Eyes latching on to me before her hands did, Zoe's fingers dug into my arms, and she pulled me toward her open apartment door.

"What?" I spun around, searching her apartment for clues as to what was going on.

"Meg, I'm freaking out." Zoe's eyes were wide, and even though intrigue flashed in her brown irises, the overwhelming emotion I saw in them was fear.

Fifteen

Heart racing, I immediately forgot my upsetting encounter with Gavin as I turned my full attention to Zoe. "What's wrong? What happened?"

After our text conversation today, I'd thought we were good. But now, pacing in front of me, Zoe seemed anything but. Her hand pushed aside her dark curtain of bangs. "Kaden and Blake went to a party tonight. Actually, from the way you're dressed, I'd say it was the same one."

"Yeah, I saw them there." I widened my eyes at her to show what a spectacle it was.

But Zoe didn't meet my gaze as she said, "While they were gone, I used the opportunity to snoop around the office."

My heartbeat increased as I realized what that meant, especially paired with Zoe's agitated state. Had she found evidence to prove Blake was Paris's killer?

Her fingers dug into my arms again. "Meg, they have a file on me."

At that, the anticipation building in me deflated. "Oh. Of course they do. All employers do that." Zoe was a few years older than me. How did she not know that?

"Not like that," Zoe said. "It wasn't full of my employment forms. It looked like they'd had someone look into my past. They had information on my mom, even a printout of her obituary. They knew our old address in Vermont, and they had my mom's name circled with a question mark and the word *traitor* next to it."

I tried to keep my breathing steady. "Okay, that is a little weird. There's no way they knew your mom, right?" I asked carefully.

"She was a real estate agent in Vermont. She used to live here, but had nothing to do with speakeasies or bars." Zoe groaned. "I think I need to quit."

Scratching at my neck, I thought back to Addy and Ripley overhearing Kaden say he was going to look into her and Blake talking about "taking care of her."

"I think that's for the best," I said.

"But I love my job. It's the first job I've loved in forever." She argued with me as if she hadn't been the one to bring up the idea of quitting.

Before I could say anything else to Zoe, my phone rang. It was my Aunt Penny. Doing the math in my head, I realized it was morning for her. She had to know it was late here. Which meant she wouldn't call me unless it was an emergency.

"I'm sorry, I have to take this," I said, shooting Zoe an apologetic glance.

She nodded but continued to pace as I took my aunt's call.

"Penny, is everything all right?" I blurted out the question the moment I answered.

Instead of launching into a quick and terrifying breakdown of whatever emergency was happening, Penny said, "Meg, is this an okay time to talk?"

Confusion flashed through me as quickly as the questions crowding my mind. And even though Penny's question about having time to talk negated an emergency, I still needed to know why she'd called.

"Uh. Yeah." I glanced over my shoulder at Zoe. She wasn't pacing anymore, but now she seemed to be having both sides of an argument as she muttered to herself, tugging at her hair in dismay. Instead of leaving Zoe alone, I moved closer to the door of her apartment. "What's up?"

Penny cleared her throat. "I hate to do this long distance, but what else can I do? What am I, going to jump on a plane just to talk to you about this?" She fought with herself, sounding a lot like what I pictured Zoe doing in that moment, not even needing me to interject. One of her dogs barked in the background as if they could feel the tension in the air too.

"Penny, what is it?" I finally asked.

"Iris mentioned you were looking into your father, and Meg, I just ... I thought I'd stressed how much your mother did not want him involved in your life, and I'm not sure what prompted this, but I really need you to reconsider." Penny rambled when she was worried. She barely took a breath during that whole rant.

At first, and maybe it was because I was caught up in the jumble of words Penny had just spewed at me, I couldn't figure out what she was talking about. I hadn't talked to Iris about any such thing. Then my gaze moved to Zoe again to check how she was doing, and understanding washed over me.

"Oh, Penny." I let out a chuckle. "That wasn't me. My friend, Zoe, who just moved into the building doesn't know who her dad is, and we were making a plan to help her figure it out. It wasn't about me." Relief lowered my shoulders.

At the sound of her name, Zoe glanced up. I waved a dismissive hand toward her, showing her it was okay.

Penny exhaled, and I swore I could feel the relief through the phone. "Omigosh." She laughed. "Phew. Okay, well, I guess I got myself all worked up for nothing." I could picture my aunt flopping onto a chair.

"I'm sorry for worrying you. Iris must've misunderstood our conversation."

Penny snorted. "I should've known better than to take what she said after a long flight, at face value. Sorry, kid. That's on me too." She was silent for a beat. "I'm glad you're making more friends, though."

I glanced over at Zoe and smiled. "Me too. Zoe and I bonded over the fact that our moms are both gone, and neither of us knows our dads. Unlike me"—I made sure I emphasized that phrase—"she really wants to figure out who her dad is. She's feeling the need for family."

"Well, she's got a great start if she's moved into the Morrisey." Penny seemed to lose herself in wistful silence for a moment. "You should ask for Iris's help looking into your friend's dad."

"Oh! You're right." With everything going on, I'd forgotten to tap Iris's librarian skills to help with the Zoe and Addy mysteries. "I'll do that. Thanks, Penny."

"Okay, kid. I'll let you go. Sorry to worry you."

"Same. Love you."

"Love you too, Megs."

I hung up and walked over to Zoe. "Sorry about that. Iris, the woman you met in the lobby with the suitcase. She's my aunt's best friend, and she must've gotten things a little mixed up when she overheard us talking the other day."

Zoe's eyes widened in understanding.

"That's actually why she was gone. She was visiting Penny in Scotland, with a bit of a layover in Iowa on the way home."

"And Penny thought you were the one who wanted to find your father?" Zoe recapped. "Was she calling to ask you not to?"

I nodded, self-conscious about how odd I know it all must seem. Zoe had been understanding yesterday when we'd talked about this at lunch, but having heard my side of the frantic conversation with my aunt, it seemed like the whole situation was making less sense to her, the more she learned.

Blunt as Zoe was, she was also a bartender, and therefore good at reading people. She could obviously tell that I didn't question the order that I keep my father out of my life, and she wasn't going to be the one to push me to do so.

"She calmed down once you told her it was me?" Zoe

asked instead of the dozens of questions she probably wanted to.

Not wanting to get into it, I said, "Yeah, and she reminded me that we should ask Iris to help us with the search for information about your dad."

"Oh, right. You mentioned that. We've just had a lot of other stuff on our minds." Zoe's frown returned. "Back to the *to quit or not to quit* question. What do you think?"

Pulling in a chestful of air, I said, "Zoe, I can't tell you what to do there. You've got to do what you think is right."

"What would you do?"

I gave her my most serious stare. "Having been in the same room with a murderer before, I can tell you I'd do everything in my power not to have that happen again."

Zoe nodded, but the faraway look in her eyes made me worried. Before I left, she repeated the information about her mother and what she knew about her father, and I texted it to Iris so she could start looking in the morning.

After that, I dragged myself across the hall, looking forward to getting out of the costume. But as I peeled out of the heavy, beaded dress, the weight on my shoulders didn't go away. The reason behind the sensation was hard to pinpoint, though.

Was I still worrying about the mistake I'd made with Gavin at the party? Was I concerned Zoe might not quit? Or was there a part of me that actually wanted to look into who my dad was?

THOSE UNCOMFORTABLE THOUGHTS about my dad grew in weight throughout the night, and I needed something to take my mind off questions I wasn't sure I was ready to answer. Luckily, Addy and Ripley were around when I woke up.

"How was the rest of the party?" I asked through a yawn as I padded into the kitchen to make coffee.

They shared a devious smile. "So fun," Addy said. "Where'd you go off to?"

"Yeah." Ripley floated after me. "We saw Gavin, but you were gone."

Sighing dramatically to set them up for what I was about to say, I filled them in on my altercation with Gavin and how he'd told me to leave.

Pupils growing throughout the story, Ripley was practically fuming by the end. "I'm going to push a door into his face," she grumbled.

Addy winced. "I'm sorry, Meg. That sounds like it was awful."

"Thanks, you two. But I don't really blame Gavin. He's right. I should've been honest with him." Sipping at my coffee, I added, "Oh, and when I got back, guess what else happened?" I explained the file Zoe had found when she'd gone snooping in the Stimacs' office.

Ripley's eyes widened. "Actually, that reminds me. We found out something that might be helpful. Blake Stimac vapes. We saw him outside the party, puffing away. And get this ... it smelled like peaches."

"Peach?" The word felt like lead in my stomach.

Paris's body had smelled like peaches. And the report

Ripley saw at the police station mentioned there had been sticky vape liquid spilled all over her. What if Blake had spilled some trying to inject it into her bloodstream? The information swirled around me as if it, too, were the silky smoke from one of those vape modules.

But then confusion tugged down the corners of my mouth.

"Wait. You can't smell. How'd you know his vape liquid smelled like peaches?" I gave both ghosts pointed looks.

"Someone walked by him and asked what flavor it was," Addy explained. "He told them it was peach pie."

"And that he gets it at City Vapes by the water." Ripley raised one eyebrow.

Nodding as I listened, I said, "Maybe the vape shop can help us track the peach-pie flavor back to Blake. Detective Anthony could use that as at least partial proof it could've been him."

Between the fight he'd had with Paris before she'd died, the passage from his speakeasy to the murder location, his cagey attitude when Zoe had asked about his alibi, and now learning that he vaped? It had to be him.

The ghosts agreed, and I got changed, taking my coffee in a to-go mug so I could sip while I walked. Having been up so late last night, it wasn't early by the time I left the Morrisey. The sun was shining, and the streets were full of more tourists than early morning commuters. From the array of green-and-blue jerseys all heading for the stadiums, it looked like there was a late morning soccer match. I slipped through the crowds and walked toward the ferries where the City Vapes website had listed their location.

As a nonsmoker, smoke shops fit in one of two categories in my mind. The first kind were filthy, old, covered in advertisement posters. They were visually overwhelming and looked like one might get a light stabbing to go with any tobacco products they purchased. The second category were the new, trendy shops. They had clean designs but were no more inviting since the workers inside looked poised and ready to harshly judge everything you did or said.

City Vapes fit in the latter category, and I steeled myself as I entered, knowing my smoking knowledge was already almost nonexistent. Addy couldn't enter with us, something we found out as she paused in front of the building, squinted, shrugged, and stepped forward anyway, then disappeared. My heart sank. Of the three of us, she was the only one who had any experience smoking. Ripley may have been an underaged drinker, but she'd never been a smoker.

The inside of the shop smelled like Fruity Pebbles and newly renovated building, which wasn't a surprise, considering their website had mentioned that the store was only about a year old. From the trendy wood-laminate floors to the LED strip lighting, I'd definitely been right when I'd categorized this as one of the more hoity-toity smoke shops. But to my surprise, the guy behind the counter beamed at me as I walked inside. Instead of glaring at me, already doubting my knowledge of smoking or vaping paraphernalia, he welcomed me in and asked how he could help.

I immediately relaxed, striding over to the counter. "I'm looking for a specific vape flavor I heard you sell here." I snapped my fingers. "It's something to do with peaches." I eyed Ripley as she moved behind the counter so she could see the computer screen, like we'd planned on the way there.

But instead of turning to the computer to type it in, the man faced the wall of bottles full of vape liquid. "Well, we have quite a few with peach flavoring." He twiddled his fingers as if he was going to grab the options off the display for me.

"Actually, my friend Blake Stimac is the one who told me about it. Do you think you could look up his order history and tell me what it is?" This man didn't have to know that I wasn't technically a friend of Blake's.

The man turned around. "Ah, if it's Blake, I don't need to look it up. He's a die-hard Peach Pie in the Sky guy." He chuckled at his rhyme as he scanned one of the rightmost shelves. After a moment, he clicked his tongue. "I'm afraid we're all out of it at the moment, however."

"Oh? Is it a popular flavor?" I asked.

The man tilted his head from one side to the other. "Blake and one other customer are my biggest fans of the flavor."

My interest piqued at this news. Just two customers who frequently bought that flavor specifically? That might be enough for Detective Anthony to link this to Blake.

As if he needed to answer the question about why he was out of that flavor, he walked over to his computer and typed for a moment before saying, "Ah, I see. We usually have more in stock, but we had to fill an extra, unexpected order, and it wiped out what I had in-store."

Ripley moved through the counter and peered over his shoulder.

He typed in something else as she watched. "My next batch is on order. I should have it in by"—he read off the screen—"Tuesday of next week. Did you want me to hold some for you?"

Letting out a groan of disappointment, Ripley's eyes moved from the screen to me. She checked the screen one more time before motioning to the door.

Surprised by her reaction, but clearly understanding it as a sign that it was time to leave, I said, "Oh, no. I can just remember to come in on Tuesday." I backed up, waving at the nice man. "Thank you."

"See you soon."

Ripley waited for me outside. Addy had returned. She rushed over to us as Ripley explained what she'd seen on the computer screen inside. "The person who purchased the last two orders of Peach Pie in the Sky was Paris Elliott."

Sixteen

Deflating, I suddenly realized why Ripley had reacted the way she had inside. "If the victim had that flavor on her already, it's not going to help the detective pin this on Blake," I summarized.

Ripley nodded sadly. Addy let out a quiet, "Oh."

Thrusting out a breath in my frustration, I started back toward home. The ghosts walked with me, but we were silent for the first part of the trip.

Then Addy surprised us both by saying, "So, you know when I tried to walk into the smoke shop before, but I disappeared? Well, I showed up at my old apartment this time instead of the Underground."

Ripley and I stopped.

"You what?" Ripley's shoulders stiffened.

I took out my phone so I could talk freely without looking like I was having a conversation with myself. "Addy, you're just telling us this now? That's huge."

"Really huge," Ripley agreed.

"Where's your old apartment?" I asked.

"That's the other weird thing," she admitted. "My family used to share the apartment, but it looks like the Elliott family purchased the whole building at some point since. From what I could tell as I looked around, they each took a floor. Sophia lives on the middle floor. Paris is at the top, where I used to live, and Foster has the first floor." She pressed her lips forward as if that was just interesting instead of monumental news.

I narrowed my eyes. "Why would you show up there instead?"

"We passed by the street on our way to the vape shop, and it made me wonder about my old apartment." She shrugged. "Maybe I just manifested there because it had been on my mind."

Ripley shook her head, slowly at first, and then the motion gained movement. "No, no. This is something." She snapped her fingers, then spun to look at me. "Megs, remember with Clark. He showed up at your apartment because the universe knew you could help him with his unfinished business."

I nodded in the same way, gaining speed as I understood. "Yes, there's a reason you showed up at Paris's apartment, Addy. It must be linked with your unfinished business. You need to go back. Look around."

Addy's expression bordered on panic as she looked between Ripley and me. "But ... I don't know what my unfinished business is. What do I even look for?"

I couldn't help her there.

"Just look around. See what stands out," Ripley suggested.

Seeing Addy didn't seem any more enthusiastic about the idea, I added, "You said it used to be your place. You can search for anything you recognize. Anything connected to you."

"Okay." Addy winced. "And you're sure neither of you can come with me?"

Ripley jabbed a thumb at me. "I can only go if Megs goes."

"And I don't think they'll let me inside," I said. "Sorry."

"Right. Okay. I'll see what I can find." She gave us a resigned smile before disappearing.

Ripley and I headed back to the Morrisey. As much fun as it had been to have Addy around lately, it was nice to fall into our normal routine. I ate some lunch and then put on our favorite grunge mix while I worked on touching up my two flapper-girl paintings and then started a third one. Rip hung out on the couch, legs kicked up on the side as she waited for Addy to return. Given how reluctant she'd seemed to poke around, I figured she'd come right back, but a few hours passed, and she was still gone.

Just as I was contemplating taking a break from painting, there was a knock on my door. I opened it to see Iris.

"Meg, I found something on your friend," she said as she moved past me into the apartment.

Her gaze stopped on the painting I was working on in the corner, and a hint of a grin played at her mouth for a moment, but whatever information she'd found must've been good because she turned back to me, eyes alight.

"That was quick." I'd only given her the information last night.

"It was more fun than catching up on all my paperwork from being gone so long. I didn't find much, yet, but the little tidbits I have found are so interesting. I just had to share. Don't worry, I'll be quick." She gestured for me to leave my door open.

"Did you find Zoe's dad?" I asked, my gaze shooting across the hall to Zoe's closed door.

Iris sighed. "Not yet, but her mother changed their last name when Zoe was only a year old. I can't figure out what it was before it was Davis, but there's definitely no record of them before that time."

"Huh," I said, an incredibly calm word for the tumult of feelings rushing through me.

Was Zoe not who she said she was? Had Ripley been right about her, after all? I couldn't bring myself to meet Ripley's gaze.

Iris patted my hand. "Anyway, I'll keep looking tomorrow, but I just had to let you know."

"Thanks," I said, giving her a wan smile. But as my neighbor bustled out of my apartment, I couldn't share in her excitement. This meant that maybe I'd been wrong about my new friend.

To her credit, and maybe because we'd just come out of one of our bigger fights in the twenty-four years we'd known each other, Ripley stayed silent about the Zoe information. I lost myself in more painting, not able to think through what that meant or worry about Addy and how her search through her old apartment was going. A while later, when I was cleaning up after painting, Ripley suggested a movie, and I didn't fight her. There was still too much to process, and it felt good to think about something else for a while.

Unfortunately, that didn't last for more than an hour. I knew it wasn't possible for Zoe to know about what Iris told me, but when my phone rang around ten that night, I worried for a moment that she could read my mind and knew I'd learned something shady about her past.

Pausing the movie, I tried to keep any tentativeness from my tone as I answered the call. "Hey, what's up?" I asked.

I was met with silence.

"Zoe? Is everything okay?" Worry engulfed me as quickly as the 1889 fire had decimated downtown Seattle.

I'd forgotten to check whether she'd decided to go back to work or not. Had something happened? I felt awful. Here I was, worrying that she might be lying to me, and she could be in trouble. Ripley sat forward, watching me intently.

I raised the volume on my phone, wondering if it was down too low and I couldn't hear her. But the volume bar couldn't go any higher. A shaky breath rattled through the line.

"Zoe, come on. You're worrying me." There was no chance that I was hiding the panic in my voice anymore. I looked at Ripley, who gave me a curt nod. "That's it, I'm coming down. I can be there in a minute. Are you hurt?" It was toward the end of her shift, but she should still be at work, if she'd even gone. But with no further information, that was where I had to start.

Just as I was about to send Ripley down to the bar to

make sure Zoe was okay, and rush after her myself, she finally said something. But it didn't help to assuage my fears.

"No. I'm fine. Everything is okay. I'm not hurt," Zoe whispered.

"Wait. Why are you whispering? Where are you?"

"Well..." Her breath came in loud pants, like she was holding the phone right up to her mouth.

My stomach flipped.

"Zoe, what have you done?"

"Blake was acting super weird today, and then he disappeared back in the office. I told Kaden I didn't feel well and pretended to go home, but I didn't."

"Where'd you go instead?" I asked, even though I had a horrible feeling I knew where.

"I checked the office, but Blake wasn't here. The closet door was open, though, and Meg, you won't believe it. There's a secret passage. I think it leads to the Underground. I'm going to follow him."

She was in the closet, about to take the passage into the Underground ... with the prime suspect in Paris's murder. The information we'd found out at the smoke shop meant we couldn't easily trace the peach vape back to Blake, but it didn't mean he was out as a suspect.

"Zoe," I blurted out. "Don't go in there."

If I knew anything from my time down there, Zoe would lose reception once she walked through.

But I didn't get any response.

And then the call dropped. I met Ripley's gaze with a wild one.

"I'll go see what I can find out." And with that, she disappeared.

I sprang into action, grabbing my phone and my keys as I raced from my apartment. Against my usual judgment, I took the elevator, glad for once when it jerked into movement before I'd quite gotten my balance. I had a feeling every second counted in this situation. Glancing down the main hall of the lobby when I spilled out of the elevator, I found it empty. Not a huge surprise so late at night, but I was glad for it all the same. I reached above the door and grabbed the key that would let me into the mechanical room, unlocking it with shaking fingers. Winding through the machinery, I moved to the back of the space and ducked through the police tape.

Ripley met me there. "I couldn't find either of them. It was too dark down there." She shook her head.

I didn't have time to think about what that might mean. I used my flashlight to get my bearings and to help me down the first few steps, but then I knew I needed to turn it off.

"I'm here, Megs," Ripley said. She wouldn't be able to see any better than I could in the dark, but knowing I wasn't alone was something.

It went against every single one of my survival instincts to turn off my flashlight. But unlike the first time I was making my way down into the Underground, there was something more dangerous than tripping or rats. If Blake saw me, he might hurt Zoe or me. I turned the flashlight off and used just the dim light from my phone screen to make sure I didn't fall and hurt myself in the untended and uneven Underground.

I wanted so badly to text Zoe, but I didn't dare do anything that would cause her phone to light up or make sound. I wasn't sure where she was or if the text would even go through since we were both potentially in the area with no service, but before I could think more about a text, the sound of crying reached my ears.

I stiffened. Was I too late? Had Blake hurt Zoe?

"Oh no." I rushed forward.

Unable to even see Ripley in the darkness, I ran my shin into an old pipe. Hissing out in pain, I froze as the crying stopped. There were a few moments of silence—if you didn't count the pounding sound of my heartbeat ringing in my ears—and I thought I'd gotten away with the sound.

Then a flashlight turned on and swept through the area like a spotlight, searching for a target. I ducked behind a wall and held my breath. The light moved past me without faltering. But a few yards later, it stopped.

Safe in the darkness now, I leaned out of my hiding place and peeked around the wall to see the spotlight pointing at Zoe, crouched behind a piece of rubble. She held a hand up to protect her eyes from the brightness.

"Zoe?" Blake's voice cut through the musty air of the Underground.

She crawled out of her hiding place, hands raised like he might have a gun pointed at her.

I didn't wait to see if he did. I raced forward, flicking on my flashlight as well, shining it straight at him. "Stay away from her," I said, using my most assertive tone as I sidled over to my friend.

Blake looked between the two of us, holding his hand up

to shield his eyes from the direct light. It was then that I noticed his eyes were rimmed with red, and his cheeks were wet with tears. He'd been the one crying? Not Zoe. He swiped a hand over his cheeks self-consciously.

"Were you crying?" I asked, incredulity lacing my tone. It wasn't the smartest tack to take with a potential murderer, but the last one I'd met hadn't cried when I'd confronted him. "Feeling sorry for what you did to Paris?" Zoe asked, stepping forward to stand next to me.

Confusion and hurt crisscrossed Blake's countenance. "What?" He spat out the question like it was a foul taste.

Zoe was on a roll, though. She gestured toward the secret passage. "You have a secret entrance into the Underground, where Paris's body was found. You fought with her the day before she died. Your families hate each other." She added the last sentence as if he should know how damning that was.

And he smokes peach-flavored vape, I added in my head, knowing Zoe wasn't aware of that last piece of evidence.

Blake's eyes contracted for a moment, looking like he was about to tell a scary story about two young women in a dangerous situation. But then he lowered his flashlight so it was pointed at the ground instead of at us. "I loved her," he said with a sad shake of his head.

"What?" The word burst out of me before I could consider what I was doing.

"Paris and I were in love. We were sneaking around because we knew our families wouldn't approve." He coughed out a humorless laugh. "Our stupid family feud."

"How?" was all Zoe could get out.

"We met because we started going to the same vape

shop about a year ago when a new one opened about midway between our two apartments. We even had the same favorite flavor." A reminiscent expression took over his features. "We'd seen each other before, obviously, but it felt like love the moment I saw her standing there with the last vial of my favorite vape liquid. I joked that it was yet another reason to keep the family feud going. She laughed, and we hit it off. She confessed that she hated the feud, too, that from a business standpoint it made for terrible optics."

I lowered my flashlight as well. Sophia had mentioned that Paris was all about optics.

"But you fought with her," I whispered, unable to believe what he'd told us.

He swung his head from side to side. "We got caught together by her sister. We had to do something. Luckily, Paris saw Sophia before we kissed, but we still had to explain why we were in the same part of the city. So Paris came up with a plan and started yelling at me, telling me to stay away from her." A grin pulled across his lips. "I thought it was hilarious, so I played along. I told her she was awful and that if she didn't stay away from my family, she'd be sorry."

I gasped. "So that's why Sophia thought you wanted to kill Paris."

"If you didn't kill her, then why are you down here?" Zoe crossed her arms over her chest.

"I miss her." Blake kicked at the ground with the toe of his shoe. "We were supposed to meet down here the day she was killed."

"How?" I asked. "The only entrance is locked, or she

would've had to go through the speakeasy, and I'm sure your family would notice if she stepped foot in your bar."

Blake sniffed. "I gave her the key for the door in the alley. We don't use it anymore, so I figured it would be the perfect place where we wouldn't be bothered by any of our family."

"Where were you on Sunday?" Zoe asked.

He put up his hands. "I was at a flower shop, buying flowers so I could meet her here." His head hung forward. "When I got here, the place was crawling with cops, and I..." He devolved into tears once more. "I miss her so much, and I can't even grieve because I'm supposed to hate every Elliott."

A flower shop. That would be easy enough to check. And based on the coughing Addy heard before she found me, Paris hadn't been dead for long at all by the time I found her, so his alibi might be enough.

"You don't have any idea who killed her?" I asked, knowing it might be a long shot.

Blake flinched. "None. She was perfect. I don't know who would want her gone." He began crying again.

The three of us stood in silence for a few moments, save for Blake's quiet sobs.

Zoe fidgeted in discomfort. "Sorry that I thought you were a killer, boss." She gave him a weak smile.

He dried his eyes. "It's okay. I didn't give you much of a choice with my actions." He jerked his head toward the speakeasy. "Should we get back to work?"

I looked at her, checking to make sure she felt safe. I noticed she hadn't brought up the file she'd found in their office, but maybe she would ask him about that later. Zoe dipped her chin, showing me it was okay.

"Don't worry, Megs. I'll stay and watch her." Ripley shot me a wink. I'd all but forgotten she was there.

Touching my elbow, the sign we'd come up with for me to say thank you when I couldn't talk, I turned back toward the Morrisey. I used my flashlight this time as I navigated my way back through the Underground. As I climbed back into the mechanical room, I thanked the universe that things hadn't turned out worse down there, and I made myself a promise that this would be the last time I would use that staircase.

Seventeen

I shouldn't have been surprised when Zoe came by my apartment about an hour later once she was officially done with work. Ripley followed behind, proving that she'd not only stayed with Zoe during her shift, but had also walked home with her to make sure she was safe the whole time.

"Hey, everything go okay?" I asked—a question that worked for both of them.

Ripley shot me a wide-eyed look that had a hint of an eye roll. It told me I would not believe what I was about to hear. Regardless of her thoughts, she stayed quiet and let Zoe talk as she filed into my apartment.

"Meg, I'm so sorry. I don't know what I was thinking." Hand on her forehead, Zoe said, "It turned out okay, but it could've been so dangerous. I thought he was a killer, and I followed him." She took a deep breath as if she needed a reminder that she was still alive, that her stunt earlier hadn't gotten her killed like it very well could have.

Not one to rub people's noses in their mistakes, I tried to be gentle with her, settling on, "It could've been so much worse. But at least now we know that you're safe at work, and you don't have to quit." I didn't want her to blame herself. It was over and we needed to move past it.

She pressed her lips together in obvious worry.

"Wait. You're *not* safe?" I mirrored her expression.

"No. In fact, after tonight, I have a feeling that we were looking into the wrong brother."

"You think it was Kaden?" I checked with Ripley, who inclined her head toward Zoe, telling me I should listen.

"Blake and I were talking while we were cleaning up tonight, and I asked him if he thought anyone in either of the families knew about his relationship with Paris. He said he'd suspected that Kaden knew at one point because he kept bringing up the feud, like he was reminding him why he shouldn't get involved with Paris. He said he decided later that Kaden was just thinking about the feud because of the centennial of the Elliott's gin and their upcoming party, but I think Blake was right when he said he thought Kaden found out about Blake and Paris's relationship." She swallowed. "And I think Kaden got rid of Paris so she couldn't tempt his brother away from the family."

Disappointment weighed down my lips. "So, you're still possibly working for and with a murderer?"

Zoe nodded.

But before she could say anything else or come up with another way to put herself in danger, I said, "Zoe, I think it's time we turn this over to the police. Tonight was scary enough when I thought you were in danger."

"Right. That's probably a good idea. No more scary situations like that for us." Zoe shot me an apologetic glance. "I promise. Want me to come with when you talk to the detective?" Zoe swallowed, wincing at the same time.

I squinted, thinking about the serious Detective Anthony. She probably *would* prefer to have Zoe come and tell her in person rather than hearing the story through me, but from the way Zoe asked, I could tell that she didn't actually want to come with me. It was an offer made, hoping I would turn it down. So, I did.

"Why don't I talk to her by myself at first?" I said. "Can I let her know that you're willing to come in and answer questions if she has more for you, though?"

"Oh good. Police make me nervous." She let out a strangled laugh. "But, yes, if she has questions, I can talk to her." Yawning, Zoe said, "Okay, I have to get some sleep. Let me know how everything goes tomorrow."

I told her I would as she left, heading across the hall to her apartment.

Once it was just me and Ripley again, we made a plan to visit the police headquarters building in the morning. But as I climbed the ladder up to my sleeping loft that night, I caught sight of the first painting I'd done of the twenties' girls, the one that looked like Addy. I hoped she was okay, and that she'd been gone so long because she was finding out what she needed to about her past.

After a fitful night of sleep, I left early and walked up to Fifth Avenue. But in all the excitement of the week, I'd forgotten what day it was and didn't realize it was Saturday until the headquarters door didn't budge when I pulled on it. Ripley groaned, sharing in my frustration. Working on a hunch before we gave up and went home, I called Detective Anthony's phone number, the one she'd given me during the last case she'd worked at the Morrisey. After three rings, she answered.

"Detective Anthony."

I'd been right. The woman was a workaholic. I figured she'd be there on the weekend.

"Hi, Detective. This is Meg Dawson, from the Morrisey."

"Hello, Ms. Dawson." Her tone was wary.

"I'm standing out front of the headquarters building. I forgot it was Saturday, but if you're in, I would love to talk to you about something to do with the Paris Elliott case."

There was only silence on the line for a breath or two. I almost thought she'd hung up on me.

But then she said, "I'll be right out."

From the look on the detective's face, as she unlocked the front doors and let me inside, I worried she wouldn't hear me out, but then she motioned for me to follow her back to her desk and I relaxed. I'd practiced what I was going to say to her the night before with Ripley, making sure I didn't drop any information I couldn't have known unless there was a ghost involved. As terrifying as it had been last night, Zoe's discovery of the secret passage made it so I didn't have to lie about how I knew it existed.

The headquarters building was empty and quiet, an eerie change from how it had been the last couple of times I'd seen it. Detective Anthony walked me back to her desk.

"What can I do for you?" She eyed me as she sat back in her chair and waited.

Wetting my lips, I said, "I think you should look into Kaden Stimac in Paris's murder."

To her credit, the detective didn't lean forward, though her shoulders tensed with anticipation. She motioned for me to continue.

I swallowed, meeting Detective Anthony's hard stare when I glanced up from my hands. "Through a series of events, I've discovered that Blake Stimac and Paris Elliott were sneaking around behind their families' backs, and I think Kaden found out about the relationship. I think Kaden killed Paris because he thought it was best for his brother."

The detective tapped a pen on the desk for a moment before saying, "Walk me through this series of events."

So I did. I started with explaining who Zoe was and how she had inside knowledge about the brothers since they were her bosses. Then I described the lunch Zoe and I had where Sophia said she'd seen Blake and Paris having a heated argument the day before Paris died. From the way the detective nodded as I spoke, she'd heard about the fight as well. Then I moved on to the scary circumstances in the Underground the night before, and how Blake had admitted to the relationship.

The detective scolded me for a good five minutes about following Zoe instead of calling her, but then she said, "He could be faking a relationship, hoping we won't take him seriously as a suspect."

"I thought about that too," I said. "And I guess he did as well, because he gave the name of a flower shop he was at before he was set to meet her in the Underground space next to his family's speakeasy." I gave her the name he'd told Zoe after work, knowing it would be easy to check.

Detective Anthony opened a file on her desk and scribbled down the information. "And he was the one who told you he suspects his brother killed Paris?"

Ripley, who'd been floating in the corner, listening to make sure I said everything we'd practiced, made her way over to the desk to look at what the detective had written. She probably wanted to make sure she was taking my information seriously.

Refocusing on the detective, and the question she'd asked me, I said, "No. Blake doesn't suspect his brother. I don't know if he's able to let himself believe it could've been someone so close to him, but from what he said, it sounds to me like Kaden had a great opportunity. Not only that, but he had access to the Underground through the secret tunnel."

I held my breath, waiting for the detective to tell me everything I just divulged was circumstantial and that I needed to get out. But she said, "I'll look into it. Thank you."

"Really?" I glanced at Ripley to see if she shared in my astonishment, but she was still studying something in the file on the detective's desk.

"Don't look so surprised, Ms. Dawson." The detective's lips tipped up into a smile. "We had no idea Paris and Blake were dating, so you found out more than us there. I appreciate you coming in." I could tell it took a lot out of the detective to thank me, especially when Zoe and I had been so reckless the previous night. She stood, ready to walk me outside.

"Hold up." Ripley froze, her eyes still glued to something in the folder. "Meg, ask about Addy," Ripley said quickly, showing me this meeting with the detective couldn't be over yet.

I cleared my throat. "Any news on the skeleton I found? Do you know who it belonged to?"

Detective Anthony shook her head. "We have a few leads, but after all these years, it's hard to be sure."

Ripley circled her hand in the air, telling me to buy her more time. "Ask if they found a purse."

"Did you—I mean, I thought I saw a purse next to the skeleton. That didn't have anything in it? No identifying papers?"

"No identifying papers." Detective Anthony confirmed. She slid a plastic evidence bag out of the folder. "Just some piece of paper with a cryptic message written on it."

"Hmmm..." I looked at Ripley, but she was too focused on whatever was in the plastic bag on the desk to give me any more cues to keep the conversation going. "Weird."

"I can't remember all of this, Meg." Ripley's tone shook with frustration. "It's not actual words, just a jumble of letters and numbers." Her gaze shot over to me. "I need you to take a picture of it."

I almost blurted out "a picture?" But the detective was already looking at me like my behavior was concerning her.

Knowing I would need to come up with something else

to talk about, I remembered Gavin. "Oh, I wanted to let you know, my friend Laurence knows a guy who works for the historical society. He might be able to help with the history part."

I didn't dwell on the way the detective's eyes lit up at the mention of Laurie.

"Good. Keep her talking. I'll create a distraction." Ripley scanned the office, creating a plan. At least, I hoped there was a plan.

Detective Anthony held a pad of paper and a pen toward me. Seeing my opportunity, I clumsily grabbed at it, causing it to fall to the floor. The detective bent to retrieve the items, and I shot Ripley a wide-eyed look that told her she needed to act now.

Ripley raced over to the water cooler in the corner, holding her hands out as she shot ghostly energy toward it. It tottered once, but Ripley hit it again with a fresh surge of energy, and it fell on its side, the water bottle dislodging from the tower. Water glugged out of the opening, spilling onto the floor.

Jumping at the noise as she held the pad of paper toward me again, Detective Anthony turned to watch the destruction. She raced over, trying to contain the mess. Fingers shaking, I pulled out my phone and covered the distance between me and the detective's desk in one long stride.

I snapped a picture, then another when I saw the plastic bag the old note was contained inside had reflected the light, marring the message in the first picture I'd taken. Flattening my hand over the bag worked to get rid of the light patterns, and I snapped another picture.

Because I was alone, and the detective was still occupied, I picked up the bag and flipped it over to make sure there was nothing on the back.

There was. A single word was scrawled in different handwriting. *Blackberry.* But I wasn't going to be able to take a picture of that because the detective was walking toward me. She focused on the piece of evidence in my hand.

I cackled nervously. "Oh. This fell." An idea clicked in my brain and I set it back on her desk. "When you rushed over, it just flew right onto the floor." I flourished my hand to mime the floating motion.

The detective glanced at my phone. She didn't need to verbalize her questions; they were clearly written in her tight posture and narrowed gaze.

"Oh, I'd just realized that I didn't know Gavin's number, so I was checking it in my phone." Grabbing the pen and paper I'd abandoned a few moments before, I pulled up Gavin's number and wrote it on the pad of paper.

The whole thing probably only took seconds, but it seemed like an eternity as I wrote without daring to look up at the rightly suspicious detective who was still glaring at me.

Setting the pen on the notepad with the finality of hands slapping down on knees, I said, "Well, now that you've got that, I'll get out of your hair."

The detective didn't say a word, following me as I scooted around the desk and skirted around the water still pooling on the floor. A quick mop would take care of the mess, however, so I didn't feel too bad as she opened the door and relocked it behind me.

Once we were outside, I fished my earbuds from my

purse and stuck them in my ears so I could talk to Ripley freely. After using so much energy, my ghostly friend was in the definite throes of "going sketchy," as she called it. Her body, which usually appeared like any living person, to my eyes, was transparent, much like Addy got when we traveled too far from her usual haunts.

"It has to be a code, don't you think?" I looked at the screen where I'd finally gotten a better picture that wasn't distorted by the fluorescent lights of the station reflecting off the bag. "And it was in Addy's purse when she died," I mused, trying to think of what it could mean.

"I wish Addy was back so we could ask her," Ripley said, concern marring her features. Her words came out at half speed and distant sounding, like it took a lot of effort to get out the sentence. Another side effect of using so much of her ghostly energy.

"Me too. But we don't even know where her old building is." Stopping, I held up a finger. "But we have access to Paris's pictures. Maybe there's a clue there."

Tucking myself up against the nearest building so I wouldn't be in the way of the foot traffic on the sidewalk, I pulled up Paris's social media accounts—which thankfully hadn't been removed—and clicked on her pictures. They opened in front of me in a tile pattern. I scanned through the lot, looking for any taken in an apartment.

"There," Ripley said, pointing a slow and transparent finger at the bottom right corner from where she hovered over my shoulder.

Sure enough, there was a picture of a beautiful fall day out her apartment window. "Hey, I recognize that tree."

"I do too," Ripley said. "I know just what street she's on."

"But you can't go inside," I said. "Do you need me to get invited in so we can find her?"

Slowly shaking her head, Ripley said, "Let me try first. Go home, and I'll let you know if I need you."

We split up. I jogged across the street and entered the Morrisey, still staring at my phone screen.

"Whatcha looking at there, doll?" The scratchy voice came from the seating area directly to the right once I entered the building lobby, but it wasn't a male voice, as I expected from the Conversationalists.

When I glanced up, Opal Halifax blinked back at me. Art and Darius weren't around, but she sat there in her usual seat, a book of word puzzles open on her lap.

"Oh. Hey, Opal." I walked forward and plopped next to her on the couch. "I'm honestly not sure what I'm looking at. It's kind of a jumble of letters and numbers."

At that, her eyes lit up and she set down her book. "That sounds like a puzzle. May I see?"

I hesitated, not sure if I wanted to show her the evidence that I'd stolen a picture of from the police station. But, other than the slight shine of the plastic bag covering the old letter, there weren't any identifying markers that would tell her it was evidence in a century-old murder investigation.

"Uh, sure." I handed over the phone just as Ripley and Addy appeared in the lobby.

"This was in my purse? Exciting." Addy rubbed her hands together as she leaned forward.

Opal peered at the screen, pinching at the picture to enlarge it. "You've got a cypher puzzle here, my dear."

I was just about to let defeat slump my shoulders forward when I glanced from the phone to the puzzle book sitting in Opal's lap. I thought back to the myriad of different puzzles I'd seen her working on since she moved in.

"Do you know how to solve one of these?" I asked.

Her eyes sparkled. "I thought you'd never ask."

Eighteen

"Do you have any paper on you?" Opal asked, before snapping her fingers and flipping to the end of her puzzle book. "Never mind, let's just use this."

Carefully, the woman wrote out the alphabet. She drew a line under it and then created vertical lines in between each letter. I looked over her shoulder as she worked, glad she was helping. I didn't have the faintest idea of where to start. My ghostly friends floated behind us as well, peering at the screen.

"Okay, first things first. We need to look for patterns." Opal's blue eyes pored over my phone screen. "I think this could be a recipe of some sort. Don't you?"

My shoulders lifted toward my ears. I wasn't sure.

"See?" She poked a knobby finger at the screen, where there were numbers at the start of each line. "Three of something. One of something else. I think this long word here might be tablespoon. Let me try it out." She scratched something on the other side of the page, eyes flashing up to meet mine when they matched up. "Okay, let me try inputting these letters into the cypher."

In the space underneath the original alphabet, she placed a T under the G, an A under the Z, a B under the Y, and so on until she'd used up all the letters in tablespoon. Sticking her tongue out the side of her mouth, Opal worked quickly. Her pen scratched at the page, jotting down the different letters she knew.

"Ah, I think this one is cardamom!" She snapped the pen down on the paper, only pausing for a moment to celebrate before getting back to work.

"Could that word be fennel?" Ripley asked from over Opal's shoulder.

I checked with Opal, who looked like she wanted to kiss me. "I think it is!" Excitement practically leaked from her body.

When we had about half of the words decoded, Addy gasped. I glanced over at the ghost, wondering what she saw.

Opal checked over her shoulder as well, and for a moment I wondered if she'd heard Addy. Then I realized she was just looking at where I was staring.

"Sorry, I thought I saw something weird outside." I turned back to the puzzle.

Opal did too. She tilted her head at the paper. "Oh, they can't be serious." She clucked her tongue in disappointment. Looking up at me, she said, "They just used the alphabet backwards. That's not very clever at all."

With that last clue, Opal decoded the rest of what was now obviously a recipe.

"It's a recipe for gin," Addy whispered. "I'd recognize those botanicals anywhere."

"Really?" Ripley looked from the recipe to her.

"My dad was the one who made it." Addy straightened her shoulders proudly.

"Then why does it say *Stimac Family Gin Recipe* at the top?" Ripley's finger shook as she pointed at the finished cypher on Opal's lap.

We'd all just attended the Elliott family Centennial Gin party and seen this very list of ingredients. And then there'd been the fight where the Stimacs had accused the Elliotts of stealing their family recipe. This seemed to be proof that they were right.

Addy gasped. "That was in my purse? I was the one who stole it?" She backed up, accidentally stepping through Ronny Arbury who was walking through the lobby. He shivered, but Addy didn't seem to notice. Her mouth hung open. "I started the feud?"

Seeing things slipping into dangerous territory, fast, I got up from the couch, tucking my phone into my pocket. "Thank you, Opal. I, uh, I have to go home now. May I take this?" I motioned to the recipe in her lap.

The woman ripped it out of her book and handed it over. Her face was tight with worry as she took in my frantic movements and obvious discomfort, but she didn't stop me as I turned to leave.

Addy was in a trance, talking to herself as she slowly shook her head. "That's why I showed up at Paris's apartment. I'm the reason she died because I stole the recipe that started the feud. It's all my fault." Tears careened down her ghostly cheeks.

Ripley motioned to the stairwell, hoping she'd join us upstairs. But when I opened the door, Addy stopped.

"No. I can't hang out with you two anymore. I don't deserve to. I did this and I have to fix it." Her lip trembled.

"Excuse me, Meg." Wendell Underwood came up behind me, hoping to enter the stairwell I was blocking.

I jumped at first, not having seen him, and then stepped aside so he could pass by. I cringed as footsteps sounded in the stairwell. It was a sunny Saturday and the building was bustling. I couldn't say anything with so many residents around. It was up to Ripley to talk Addy through this.

"You didn't find anything at Paris's?" Ripley asked softly.

Addy shook her head, sniffling. "Not a thing. I looked all day yesterday. I'm sorry. I've failed you. I've failed my family. I never deserved to come out from the darkness downstairs."

And with that, she disappeared.

I stepped toward the mechanical room doorway, about to grab for the hidden key on top of the frame so I could go after her, but Art and Darius stepped out of the elevator, heading toward their regular spot by the door. To avoid getting into a conversation with them, I stepped inside the stairwell.

Ripley followed me. "I'll go talk to her."

I gave her a reluctant nod. Ripley disappeared, and I started up the stairs. By the time I reached the fifth floor and unlocked the apartment, Ripley was there waiting for me.

Just Ripley.

"No luck?" I asked through a frustrated exhale.

"She won't listen. She just keeps repeating how it's all her fault, how she's responsible for the fighting and the deaths, and how she's sure one of the Stimacs caught her stealing and killed her."

"There's no way she stole the recipe on purpose." I paced through the studio.

"I know, but that's what she seems to think. How can we possibly convince her otherwise?" Ripley sank onto the couch.

"There has to be someone who knows what happened back then, who can convince her she didn't have that recipe because she was stealing it." I continued to pace. "What about Rooftop Rachel?" We couldn't be sure based on the nightgown she wore, but it was possible that the silent ghost on the roof might've been from the same time period as Addy.

"No go," Ripley said. "Addy and I were up there the other day, and we couldn't get her to talk to either of us."

I vented my irritation through a long exhale even though Rooftop Rachel never talked, so I wasn't sure why I'd expected this time to be different.

Ripley joined in my pacing, following behind as I walked through my frustration, willing my brain to come up with something. Suddenly I was cold all over, and I realized I'd passed right through Ripley.

But she didn't seem to mind. She was frozen on the spot, chewing on her lip.

"What? Did you think of something?"

She gave me a slow, half-hearted nod. "You're not going to like it."

I glared at her. This wasn't the time for liking or not liking things. Our friend was hurting.

"Remember when Gavin talked about the gambling den and the shootout?" When I nodded, Ripley said, "Addy mentioned she tried to get in all the time, that the Stimac guy she thought was cute spent a lot of time there."

"And?" I asked, not seeing the point.

"And she mentioned how there were two big brutes, along with a skinnier boss."

Suddenly, I was ten all over again. Penny ventured down to the basement to look for an extra dog crate another resident thought they'd stored down there, and I went to keep her company. The three ghosts were hidden at first among the piles of old furniture and storage boxes. But once they realized we were down there, they came rushing through us, knocking over things and freaking out Penny even though she couldn't see them. Ripley and I, who could see them, had been even more terrified. To that day, I could still picture their twisted, evil smirks as they chased us out of the basement.

Three of them. Two huge, hulking brutes and a skinnier, scarier boss.

"The basement ghosts?" I started shaking my head even before I finished the question.

Ripley wrinkled her nose in a way that told me that was going to remain her answer whether I liked it or not.

Holding up a hand as a clear sign it was not going to happen, I continued to shake my head for added negative effect. "There's no way I'm going down there again. I've been able to avoid them for fourteen years, and I don't plan on breaking that streak."

"I know." Ripley shivered. "I'm not saying you'll like it, but you said you were out of options. I'm merely pointing out that you're not."

"Me? Why can't you go?" I turned on her.

Ripley shook her whole body out like an athlete warming up. "Fine. I'll do it. I'll go talk to them. They can't hurt me."

Her last statement held more of a question than I was comfortable with. I'd spend a lot of time feeling bad for Ripley that ghosts couldn't touch, but this was one time I was happy that they wouldn't be able to lay a ghostly finger on my best friend.

"For Addy," she said before disappearing.

I nodded in encouragement. My stomach was in knots the moment she disappeared. I pulled Anise into my lap and wished she could talk so she could console me, tell me I hadn't been a coward for sending my friend.

But before my cat could learn to talk, Ripley returned.

Her face was a mixture of frustration and disgust. When I hardened my forehead in question, she merely shook her head, like she didn't have the words to describe what had happened.

"Let me guess. They won't talk?" My tone was flat, unimpressed.

She pressed her mouth into a thin line. "Not to me."

"What does that mean?" I whirled on her.

She grimaced.

Scooping the air in front of me, telling her to bring it on, I said, "Tell me. I can handle it." Anything for Addy, right?

"They said"—Ripley cringed—"they wanted to talk to the 'fleshy one.'" Ripley used air quotes around the phrase, as if I would've mistaken the terrifying wording as hers instead of that of the nightmarish basement ghosts.

Curling my lip, I pulled in a long breath through my nostrils. Talking with the basement ghosts might be our only chance to figure out what happened to Addy.

"Okay," I said, resigned. "I'll go." If I hadn't been wearing a tank top, I would've rolled up my sleeves to signify that I was ready to do what needed to be done to help our friend.

Ripley stepped in front of me. "I don't know, Megs. They're so creepy. Are you sure there's not another way we can figure out what really happened to her?"

"I won't be able to live with myself if we don't try. Plus, you're going to come with me."

There wasn't technically anything my ghostly companion would be able to do against the basement ghosts if they came at me again. If I'd been about to face living foes, Ripley could've wielded energy to push them back and buy me some time. Against other spirits? Nope. But these ghosts obviously didn't get out much if they called people fleshy, and I was counting on the fact that they wouldn't know the ghostly rules, much like Addy hadn't.

I ventured down, taking the stairs slowly as I prepped myself with reminders that I was brave. The steps leading from the lobby level of the stairwell to the basement were the hardest to convince my feet to travel down, but I made it. The lighting was sorely lacking down there, of course, and even with Ripley by my side, my kneecaps still shook with fear.

I tried clearing my throat, but it didn't get anyone's attention.

"Hey, losers," Ripley called into the dark space. "I brought back the *fleshy* one. Come out and talk."

We were met with a silence that seemed just as heavy and hulking as the large pieces of antique furniture or boxes full of people's possessions surrounding us. I was about to turn back, glad not to have to stay, when a scratchy whisper cut through the darkness.

"Back here. Come closer."

There was a hush and a throaty chuckle that sounded like evil itself rang through the basement. Looking at Ripley first, I stepped forward. Rounding a corner, I jumped and rushed backward until I ran into a stack of boxes. A mannequin stood in the corner.

"Sorry, Meg. I didn't see it the first time I came down." Ripley rushed forward to block the thing with her spirit.

I recognized the mannequin as the same one from Mr. Miller's apartment. They must've moved it down here when he died. I gulped back my fears and walked forward until I couldn't see the dreaded mannequin any longer. But once the motivation to get that creepy thing out of my line of sight was gone, I couldn't seem to convince my feet to keep moving. I froze in the middle of the basement.

Ripley stood next to me, glancing at my feet in question.

I shook my head, showing her I couldn't move any farther. Instead, I called out, "I'm here. You need to meet me halfway." My voice wavered, doing a terrible job of hiding my fear.

But that fear was nothing compared to the stab of terror that cleaved me in two when three men stepped out of the shadows and into the main walkway about twenty feet away from me.

My heartbeat spiked, and I felt slightly woozy as I took them in. One of the men was smaller, not in height—all three of them were quite tall—but two of them were brutishly large.

"Is this the same one with the aunt who had the great gams?" one bouncer asked, throwing a ghostly elbow at his counterpart.

"She's grown up." He looked me up and down. "Got her aunt's gams, looks like."

Disgust overcame the fear that was taking over my senses, and I snorted. "Gross."

"Hear that, Norman? She thinks we're gross." The one on the left giggled a high-pitched cackle.

Norman? Ripley and I shared a questioning glance.

"Oh, yeah?" Norman asked, stepping forward. "We'll show her gross, Herbert."

Any humor I found in the name Herbert was quelled by Herbert joining Norman as he stalked toward me. I didn't want to know what he had in mind to convince me how gross they truly were.

Ripley stepped in front of me. She glanced back, eyes wide, her horrified expression telling me to be ready to run. But before I could, Herbert and Norman came to a stop, bent forward, and belched in my direction. They broke into a fit of giggles.

These were the guys we'd feared my whole life? Burping? They were goofs.

"Silence." The third man's voice cut through their laughter, and the two straightened their spines as they stopped all noise in an instant.

It was then that I realized that I'd been wrong. These men weren't inherently terrifying, but they would do whatever their boss instructed them to do, and that made them dangerous. I couldn't let my guard down.

"You'll have to excuse me for my friends." The third one stepped forward, his voice like silk ... right before it wraps around your neck and tightens. His voice was the evil-sounding one that had called me forward. "They don't see many people in the flesh." His tongue curled around the last word.

Every cell in my body screamed for me to run away, but I thought of Addy, and I wanted so much for her to be at peace. So, I took a deep breath and stepped one foot closer to them.

"I need to know if you have any information about what happened to Addison Elliott the night she died. I found her body just over there." I gestured to the wall, knowing they would be able to picture what it had looked like down here before it had been closed off like it was now. "And I hear the three of you once knew everything that happened in this section of the Underground." I didn't miss that Norman's eyebrows lifted in recognition when I said Addy's name. Herbert let out a little sigh.

Despite the hope that filled me, based on the brutes' reactions, it was dashed when the boss clucked his tongue, and an evil smirk pulled at his thin lips. "Aww, little girl, we have no intention of spilling our secrets to someone like you."

Mustering all my courage, I said, "Fine, then I'll take my flesh elsewhere, along with any chance of you moving on." I crossed my arms.

Ripley let out a whoop of support from my side.

I was about to turn around, to leave, when—

"Wait."

Now it was my turn to smirk. *That's what I thought.* I turned around to face the ghost, ready to hear the truth.

Nineteen

"What do you mean, help us move on?" The boss's silky voice was taut with the possibility. The intensity of it, and the way he was leering at me, made me want to run all over again.

Instead, I swallowed and said, "Well, your spirits are stuck here. That's not normal. It means you have unfinished business before you can move on to ... wherever spirits go." I jerked my shoulders in a shrug to show them I didn't know, but I hoped they could see that anything had to be better than this. "I can help you figure out what happened."

Herbert and Norman stepped forward eagerly. Their boss whipped his arms out on each side to stop them from going any farther. And even though he couldn't physically restrain them anymore, their fear of him stopped them in their tracks.

"And what do you ask for in return?" he asked.

I wet my lips. "I just want to know if you have any information on Addison Elliott's death. She's a friend, and she's suffering, has been for a long time."

At my second mention of Addy, there was another reaction to her name. This time, however, all three of the men reacted. The boss's flinch would've been hard to catch if I hadn't been staring straight at him, but it was definitely there. No matter how scary he seemed, there was something in him that had cared for Addison Elliott. Well, or he despised her, and hearing her name reminded him of how much of a thorn in his side she was, but knowing Addy, it had to be the former.

And I was about to bet on it.

"Addy thinks she started the century-long family feud between the Elliotts and Stimacs. She's sitting in the dark right now going through the Stimacs she saw as *family,* trying to think of who could've killed her for taking their gin recipe." I stared into the boss's dark eyes, unwavering.

"Milo, she can't—" Norman started, but his boss held up a fist, shutting down whatever it was with that one move.

I readied myself to leave. He wouldn't help me. My phone buzzed in my pocket. The call was coming from Iris. My finger hovered over the accept button. I was about to tell these unhelpful ghosts that I needed to take the call, that it wasn't worth my time to wait around, when the boss cleared his throat.

"Addy was always trying to get inside my club," Milo muttered.

His use of my friend's nickname caused me to pause. I turned my attention from the phone to the ghost in front of me.

"Her father forbade me from letting her in. He paid me, in fact, to keep her out," Milo continued.

"We just had to tell her she had the wrong password each time she tried," Herbert said with a chuckle.

Ripley and I shared a revelatory look. So that was why she could never "remember" all the passwords. They convinced her that she was getting the one for the gambling hall wrong.

"Until one time when she hid around the corner while someone else gave us the password," the same bouncer said.

"Blackberry," the other added with a sigh. "I'll never forget."

My breath caught in my throat. *Blackberry*. That had been written on the back of the gin recipe. What if Addy had grabbed a random piece of paper, not knowing that it was the recipe, and written the password so she wouldn't forget it? As excited as I was about the possibility, Milo was talking again.

"It was blackberry. We couldn't deny it. And these two let her inside," he said. "So, I had to get creative."

Norman stepped forward. "We didn't mean to hurt her. We just wanted to scare her so she'd leave."

I blinked in confusion.

"The boss told us to get her out of there, so we rushed her. Yelling and screaming. You know, being scary. She screamed and ran away. She didn't see the low-hanging pipe until it was too late." Herbert shook his head.

I shivered, knowing their tactic of rushing and scaring off people all too well. It was precisely what they'd done to me that day fourteen years ago when I'd come down here with Penny.

Milo pinched at the bridge of his nose as he listened. "As you can see, it wasn't a Stimac who killed her. Just these two." He rolled his eyes.

Herbert and Norman sagged in sadness at the reminder.

"I'd say it's on you since you gave the order," I said, stepping forward. "And I'm guessing she's not the only innocent person's death you're responsible for. Which makes it completely understandable why you're still here."

"And the two of you are here because you did whatever he told you to," Ripley added. "Still do, it seems."

Milo lifted his hands as if to say there was nothing they could do about it now.

But I knew of something they could try. I turned on my heel.

"Where are you going? I thought we had a deal." Milo's voice was tight.

"We do. I'm taking you to Addy. You need to tell her all of this so she doesn't think one of the Stimacs did this to her, so she doesn't think she stole that recipe on purpose." I started for the stairs again. Even though I thought I'd figured it out with the password, blackberry, she'd be more likely to believe if she heard it straight from the source.

"You don't have to go that way." Milo's words stopped me.

I turned to look at him in question.

He jerked his head to the left. "There's a way through down here."

"I thought they closed it all off." I turned back toward him.

"They thought they did, but this building has secrets only I know." Milo lifted his eyebrows twice.

Ripley and I followed.

Like the other first stories of buildings that I'd seen sealed up in the Underground, doorways and windows had been covered with brick and concrete, but most of the original structure was untouched. They'd made sure they'd built the new structures well after the Great Fire.

I turned on my flashlight as we moved into the back of the basement where the lights became less helpful. Milo stood and pointed to a safe built directly into the stone wall.

"Oh no. Nope. There's no way I'm getting in there." I took two steps back. "I'll take my chances going around."

I could just see it now. These terrible men playing an awful trick by convincing me to climb into the safe and pushing the door closed with their ghostly energy so I was locked inside.

Milo yawned, bored with my protestations. "The back isn't fully intact. There's a hole you can climb through."

I needed to see for myself before I walked into it. Reaching forward, I grabbed at the lever, but it wouldn't budge. "How am I supposed to get into it if it's locked?"

"I know the combination," Milo said.

I waited while he told me which numbers to use and how many turns in each direction. The lock clicked, and I pushed down on the lever. It took a pull that had all my weight behind it to open the door, but I finally convinced the rusted thing to swing open. Standing away from the door, I angled my flashlight into the opening.

"See? It goes straight through," Milo told us. His brutes nodded behind him.

Ripley's shoulders straightened as she saw the same thing I did, a hole big enough to climb through that led straight into the Underground, a place I'd spent way more time than I ever wanted to.

Without overthinking it, I walked through. Remembering the rats I'd seen in the Underground, I pulled the safe door closed behind me.

"Meg, what if it latches?" Ripley rushed forward, next to me, her spirit glowing in the light of my flashlight.

"I left it unlocked, see?" I shoved the heavy door with my shoulder with a grunt, and it swung open. "As long as no one on the other side moves that lever, we're good. But we can also get out through the mechanical room staircase if we need to."

The fear in her eyes lifted away.

I walked forward until my flashlight stopped on a spirit I knew well. Addy was curled in a ball, sitting in the small closet where I'd found her skeleton. At the brightness, she looked up. I glanced over each of my shoulders to see Ripley, Milo, Herbert, and Norman standing behind me.

Addy blinked. "What's going on?"

"These guys have something to tell you," I said, hoping they would follow through with their end of the bargain.

They repeated the story they'd told me and Ripley just minutes before.

Tears dripped down Addy's cheeks as she listened.

"See, Addy? You must've grabbed that paper just to write the password on the back. You didn't know what it was." It wasn't a smiling kind of situation, but I tried to give her an encouraging look.

"And it wasn't the Stimacs who killed you. It was these goofuses." Ripley hitched a thumb toward the three men.

Tears continued to stream down her cheeks. She hiccuped. "I do remember stopping by the speakeasy office to grab something to write on. I swear I didn't know it was the recipe when I took it." Tilting her head, she turned her attention to the men. "But why did you put me in this closet?"

Milo's expression tightened. "Your father showed up, and we had to hide your body. We couldn't keep you in the gambling den, so I had these two bring you out here, knowing no one used this closet. We were going to move you, eventually, but we were all killed in the shootout before we could."

Addy snapped her fingers. "I knew my father had been going to your club. He denied it, but there wasn't any covering that rosemary smell." Her forehead wrinkled. "Was he in trouble?"

The henchmen shifted uncomfortably.

"Not at first," Milo admitted. "But he started complaining more and more about Elmer, saying they weren't seeing eye to eye, that Elmer wasn't treating him like a partner. One night, he ran out of money and tried to use the gin recipe as collateral." Milo clicked his tongue.

"The boss *had* to tell Elmer," Herbert said.

Norman nodded. "Elmer paid us to keep him informed."

We waited for Milo to deny it, but he simply added, "More than your father paid me to keep you away," as if it was out of his control.

Addy's eyes went wide. "So, Elmer thought my dad was really trying to sell the gin recipe?"

"Yes," Milo said. "He told me he was going to write it in code, destroy the original, and see how Charles liked that."

Addy snorted. "Daddy knew that recipe by heart. He didn't need the piece of paper."

"I tried telling that to Elmer, but he was blind with rage when even the coded recipe disappeared." Milo frowned. "I didn't know you had it. After you went missing, Elmer assumed you'd run away with it, fired your father, and went back on their agreement about being equal partners in their business." Milo nodded toward the building the Stimacs still owned.

"And that's what started the feud." Ripley's voice was small in the mostly dark area.

Addy sniffed. "Yeah, it was still me."

Milo, terrifying and unfeeling as he'd seemed, stepped forward, leaning down until he was closer to Addy's level. "No, little darling. You were a bright butterfly in that dark world we'd created. You made everyone's day better just by talking to us. Do not blame yourself for getting caught up in the greedy dealings of people who didn't have half the soul you do. The feud between your families had been brewing longer than that gin your father used to make. Elmer became paranoid, and your father fell right along with him."

The kindness Milo displayed in that moment surprised me. But Addy looked up into his eyes, and a small amount of happiness touched her lips as she gave him a smile and sniffed away a last tear.

"I'll stay down here forever in shame, knowing I took your light from the world," Milo whispered.

"Us too," Herbert and Norman muttered.

"I thought you wanted my help in finding out why you're still here?" I asked.

Milo let out another one of those silky, dangerous laughs. "I know very well why I'm here, and I doubt I'll be leaving anytime soon." His chest swelled as if with pride, or maybe just acceptance. "My purgatory is spending the rest of eternity in that dusty basement with these two oafs."

"I know this is a nice, touchy-feely moment, but does anyone else find it weird that Addy's still here?" Ripley said under her breath, obviously feeling awkward being the one to bring it up.

Addy stood up, dusting herself off even though she didn't need to. "Whether I meant to, I helped start the feud. And I think it's up to me to finish it. If we have any hope of doing that, we have to figure out who killed Paris." She nodded resolutely.

Ripley and I scrunched our noses in tandem. "We're not sure the truth is going to help stop the feud. Right now, our top suspect is Kaden Stimac."

Addy's mouth pinched to one side as she contemplated that. "Well, I need to try."

I promised her I would help, just as soon as I got myself out of the Underground and back into the safety of my apartment. She and Ripley disappeared once I'd climbed through the safe and locked it securely behind me. I gave one last look over my shoulder at the three ghosts in fancy suits before I turned off the light and climbed up the stairwell.

Around the third floor, my phone buzzed in my pocket. Right. The call from Iris. I'd been under the building, so whatever message she'd left was probably only just coming through now that I had service again. I pulled out my phone, but noticed that along with a voicemail, I had two texts from Gavin, of all people.

> Meg, I'm so sorry about how I acted the other night. Are you home today? I'd love to come by and explain myself.

Then, less than a minute ago, he'd sent another one.

> I'm out in front of your building.

I turned on my heel and headed downstairs, typing out a reply as I went.

> Coming down.

Conflicting thoughts swirled through my mind as I wound down the stairwell toward the lobby. On one hand, Gavin *had* been pretty dismissive of me. I'd deserved some of that for not letting him know about my connection to the Elliotts, but I hadn't expected to see him again. On the other hand, he was a good friend of Laurie's. I could at least hear him out.

As I walked through the stairwell door and into the lobby, there was a small commotion happening by the front doors.

Opal stood in front of Gavin, her thin arms splayed out

as if she were protecting him from a pack of wolves. Standing in front of her were Darius and Art, who held rolled up newspapers like they were about to swat a fly. George floated nearby, bobbing back and forth like he didn't know which side to take.

"Hey," I said as I jogged forward. "What's going on here?"

Twenty

Art and Darius whirled around to face me. The scowls they'd been wearing morphed into surprise. Their mouths hung open, but neither of them immediately spoke.

"They're worried this young man is trying to break into the building, even though he says he knows you," George told me.

Finally, Darius said, "We're just trying to follow Nancy's instructions not to let people we don't know into the building anymore."

"And then Opal goes and lets in a stranger," Art added.

Darius held up a finger. "After letting in another one of those Elliotts earlier."

Opal snorted. "I told you, I never let an Elliott in here. You two are seeing things. You need to get your glasses checked. I didn't even let this one inside. Zoe did. She told me she had to run some errands before work, but that this gentleman was a friend of Meg's and to help him find her."

"I'll believe it when Nutmeg says it." Darius lifted an eyebrow in suspicion as he looked Gavin up and down.

I placed a hand on my hip. "I know him," I admitted, but I couldn't get mad at the Conversationalists for trying to do a better job of protecting the building. "Thank you for checking, though." I walked past them, planting a light kiss on each of their cheeks. "And thank you for protecting him, Opal." I winked at her as she stepped aside and I stood in front of Gavin.

Eyes wide, Gavin pushed back his shoulders. "Uh, thanks for coming, Meg." His gaze drifted across the lobby. "Is there a more private place we can talk?"

Opal whistled but pretended to go back to solving her puzzles as she settled back onto the couch.

"Yes, you can come up to my place." Anything was better than trying to talk here, with so many sets of eyes on us. Taking the elevator because I didn't feel like making Gavin climb all five flights, I turned to him. "So, what's up?" I didn't cross my arms in front of me, but I could feel the coldness in my question.

Gavin must have too, because he flinched. "I shouldn't have yelled at you the other night. I came to apologize. I also wanted to let you know everything worked out how it was supposed to, so there are no hard feelings."

The elevator dinged open, spitting us out onto the fifth floor. "What do you mean?" I asked as I unlocked my place and invited him inside. Addy and Ripley waited for me, their expressions full of questions I couldn't answer as I entered. I shot them both wide-eyed looks before I turned back to face

Gavin and gestured for him to sit as I settled onto the couch next to Ani.

Gavin's eyes sparkled. "We got back the donation."

I blinked. "What donation?"

"I thought..." He shook his head. "Laurie didn't tell you?"

"I haven't talked to Laurie in days," I admitted, feeling that fact like a punch to the gut. We'd both been busy, I rationalized.

"About a week ago, the Elliotts pulled their funding from the historical society." Gavin heaved out a sigh. "It was why I had to go to the ball last minute. No one was sick. My boss wanted me to try appealing to them one more time to see if they'd reconsider. Given that I'm the newest hire, and this job means everything to me, I volunteered. And with Paris out of the way, they did." He beamed.

Confusion inched along my skin, making me shiver. "What do you mean, with Paris *out of the way*?"

"She was the one who told us they wouldn't be giving the donation anymore," he explained. "And when I learned Boutique Liquor was getting a second chance now that Paris was out of the picture, I figured we might get the same deal."

I tried to wrap my mind around what was happening.

"It's why I freaked out on you when I found out the Elliotts didn't like you. I couldn't have anything ruin what I'd just worked so hard to get back," he continued to explain even though I'd said nothing in response to his last statement.

"You knew Boutique Liquor was getting a second chance?" I narrowed my eyes at him.

Gavin wet his lips. "Yeah, I told you that."

Shaking my head slowly, I said, "No. You were surprised that they were there because Paris had so publicly cut ties with them and embarrassed them."

Ripley and Addy leaned closer, picking up on my confusion.

"Oh, I must've gotten that muddled because I was so nervous about approaching Foster." Gavin waved a hand in my direction. "It's why I had to calm my nerves and get some fresh air. I needed to psych myself up."

I remembered that. He'd called it "fresh air" but had pulled out that vape pen. It hadn't seemed like a red flag then. Now that I knew he had cause to get rid of Paris, it was confirmation that he had access to the murder weapon.

Smiling as sweetly as I could, I grasped my hands together in my lap to keep them from shaking. I remembered Gavin talking about how everyone else at the historical society had been there for ages. He was the newest employee, the one who would get cut if funding dried up. He'd said that his job meant everything to him. Would he kill to keep it?

"Well, don't worry about it at all," I said as I moved toward the door. "I really appreciate you coming here to apologize, though. I'm sorry I wasn't up front about my past run-ins with the Elliotts too."

Gavin hesitated, causing my pulse to skyrocket. Would he refuse to leave? Had I invited a potential killer into my apartment? Ripley must've seen the fear in my face, because she bit down on her lip, squeezed her eyes shut, and then passed through Gavin repeatedly. Addy, getting the hint, did the same.

A shiver passed down Gavin's spine, and he rubbed his palms up and down his arms. "Oh man. I just got the worst chill."

I laughed, tight and awkward. "Weird. It's super hot out today, and all the heat just collects up here on the fifth floor. Maybe you're getting sick." Getting past the ickiness I felt at touching him, I placed a hand on his back and nudged him toward the door. "You've had a stressful week. You should go home and get some rest."

He looked dazed as I flung open the door and walked outside with him. Stepping back so he was standing in the hallway alone, I grabbed on to my door and held it tight to me so it was just my head sticking out.

"Sorry, don't mean to kick you out. I just can't afford to get sick right now. You understand, right? Bye." Shutting the door, I held the knob with shaking fingers, knowing he would hear if I clicked the lock with him standing there.

I peered through the peephole, counting my breaths as he stood in the hall and rubbed at the back of his neck in confusion. But then he finally started toward the elevator. A large breath whooshed out of me as I threw the lock on the door and headed to the couch.

"Dude, was it just me or does Gavin totally sound like he could've been the one to kill Paris?" Ripley said, stating the obvious.

Eyes flashing to her, I said, "Totally. But it's Kaden, right? It has to be Kaden. We gave the detective all the info she would need to go after Kaden Stimac, just like Blake pointed out to us."

"Or, Kaden had nothing to do with it, and Gavin's the

one who killed her so he could get back the Elliotts' money," Ripley said.

"I think it all depends on how much my family was giving them," Addy chimed in. When we both blinked at her, she added, "If the amount was small, it wouldn't have been enough to shut down his work. Maybe it was more of an inconvenience."

"But if the donation was large, and his job might've been cut, that would be a motive." I saw where she was going.

"We didn't ask him that before we kicked him out," Ripley observed.

Chewing on my lip, I said, "Yeah, I'm realizing that now."

"You could go after him," Addy suggested.

But the thought of being around him again made my skin tingle with discomfort. Snapping my fingers, I said, "I have a safer idea." Then I started counting on my fingers.

Ripley realized what I was doing because she said, "Ask Laurie. Good call. What time is it over there?"

I squinted as I finished counting. "Six in the morning?" It was a question because I didn't know if that was an unreasonable time to call. He'd called me about this same time the other day, though.

"He's a professional guy. He'll be up by now." Ripley nodded in assurance. "Call him."

I didn't overthink it. Pulling up our last video conversation, I pressed on his name, and a new video call began. My heart was in my throat during all four of the rings, but then the wonderful chime that told me he'd picked up the call sounded. Laurie's hand blocked his smiling face for a moment as he situated the camera on what seemed to be a bathroom mirror, based on the tiled walls in the background. Once the phone was steady, his fingers moved to the tie he'd been tightening when I'd called.

"Hey." The word was covered in a laugh. "When I said you have to call next, I didn't think it would be this early."

"Night owl, remember?" I said with a lightness I didn't feel. "I just have something quick to ask you and then I'll let you go."

He nodded, but before I could jump in, he said, "Oh, did Gavin talk to you?"

"He did," I drawled.

Any tightness in Laurie's expression relaxed. "Good. I told him he should. He messaged me yesterday, saying he felt terrible about how things had gone at some party." Laurie's face screwed up into a sly grin. "I didn't ask too many questions because I was at work, but … did you and Gavin go to some sort of ball together?"

Smirking at his playfulness, I laughed. "It was a bootlegger's ball, and it was all for research into the case. Why? Were you jealous?"

He finished with his tie and tilted his head. "Maybe a little." He coughed. "Or a lot."

"You look like you're off to a similarly fancy place right now," I said, taking the time to appreciate how handsome he looked in the dark suit, white shirt, and tie.

"Just a meeting, but it's with some important people, so I've got to look nice."

"You always look nice," I said, surprising myself with my candor.

Addy let out an excited squeal. Ripley clapped her fingertips together proudly in my direction.

Laurie's mouth tugged into that sexy half smile, and he dipped his head forward. "Thanks. Nothing compared to you, or how great you must've looked dressed up for a ball." He cleared his throat. "Anyway, you had a question for me, and I keep changing the subject."

I blinked. Right. I'd gotten distracted by Laurie's smile. "Yeah, it's about Gavin, actually. When he was texting with you, did he mention why he needed to apologize?"

There was a wariness in Laurie's tone as he said, "He said he was stressing about something at work and snapped at you. Was that not it?" Laurie's jaw tightened.

"That was it. He told you the truth. I'm just a little confused about the work thing. Did he explain it to you at all?"

"He just said a big donor for the historical society had pulled their funding, and it was going to either be him getting them back or losing his job." Laurie lifted his large shoulders in a shrug.

My eyelids fluttered closed. That was exactly what I *didn't* want to hear.

"What? Is that bad?" Laurie asked, guessing by my reaction.

"Tread carefully here, Megs," Ripley warned. "This is his friend."

I opened my eyes to see Laurie waiting for my answer. "I think Gavin might be more involved in this Underground stuff than we first thought."

"The history?" Laurie wasn't understanding.

Cringing, I said, "The murder. The person who pulled the funding is the one who died. With her out of the way, he was able to save his job."

Laurie ran a hand over his face, blinking as if he was suddenly exhausted. It *was* six in the morning, so maybe he was. And I'd just dropped this bomb on him about an old friend.

"I think you're wrong."

His words took me by surprise. "What do you mean?"

"Gavin wouldn't hurt anyone." Laurie's eyebrows slanted, creating harsh lines on his normally kind face. "Correlation doesn't mean causation, Meg. I think you're jumping to a conclusion because you're frustrated."

"Laurie, he vapes. Paris was killed with an overdose of nicotine because someone injected vape liquid into her veins." Anger flared inside me at his inability to see what I so clearly could. "I'm guessing they meant for no one to find her for a while, that they might think she'd died of natural circumstances by the time they found her body, but I interrupted them when I came into the Underground that day and they left the syringe in her neck." I was rambling.

"I don't see it." He checked his watch. "And I've really got to go, or I'm going to be late for my meeting. I'm sorry."

Gritting my teeth, I exhaled through my nose. "Fine. Good luck." I hung up the call before he could say anything else.

Frustration surrounding Laurie wasn't necessarily a new sensation. I'd spent my whole life so far wishing we could be more than just friends, but it was more about circumstances.

Those feelings had never been directed at him before. This was new, and I hated it.

Tossing my phone onto the couch, I paced through the apartment.

"Meg," Addy said, stepping forward. "Are you okay?"

I shut my eyes. "Yeah, Addy. I'm great. I just fought with the guy I've loved my whole life, and he's five thousand miles away. I'm perfect."

"Don't bite her head off just because you didn't handle that well," Ripley snapped back.

Whipping around to look at her, I opened my eyes. "What's that supposed to mean?"

She cocked her hip. "I told you to tread lightly, yet you proceeded to burst into that conversation like a Hummer on a bumper-car track," she said flatly.

"How was I supposed to tell him I think his friend might be a killer? There's no good way to say that." I threw my hands in the air.

"Come on, Addy. I need some fresh air. Let's go up to the roof and give Meg some room to cool off." Ripley's words were sharp, and she glared at me until the moment she disappeared. Addy followed a second after.

Anise blinked up at me from where she was on the couch. Even she looked disappointed. I pulled a few deep breaths through my nose, feeling the air cool my heated thoughts. Maybe I *had* handled that poorly. Shaking my head, I went to find Addy and Ripley on the roof, so I could apologize.

But as I opened the door to my apartment, ready to jog up the flight of stairs leading to the roof, I froze.

A man with dark hair stood in the hallway. At first, fear gripped me, thinking it was Gavin. Had he come back? Never left?

But then the man turned around, and I recognized him. Blake Stimac.

Twenty-One

"Blake?" I blinked in surprise at seeing the man standing in the fifth-floor hallway of the Morrisey.

The younger Stimac brother jumped and fidgeted with something in his back pocket for a moment before meeting my gaze. "Meg, hey."

"What are you doing here?" I looked around the hallway, as if the reason he was here might be hiding in plain sight.

"I, uh ... well, I'm here to see you." He hooked his thumbs into his belt loops, but only for a second.

"Me?" I placed a hand on my chest.

He swallowed, his manic mannerisms only growing more erratic as he swiped a hand through his hair. His gaze flicked around the fifth-floor hallway before he said, "I think I know who killed Paris."

Swallowing, I studied his face, looking for the resigned expression of a man who'd finally come to the conclusion that his brother could've killed the love of his life.

He shook his head. "I can't believe it was right in front of me all along."

There it was. Laurie was right. I'd been wrong about Gavin. If even Blake believed it was his brother, it had to be right.

I put a hand on his arm and softened my posture to match. "Hey, Blake. It's okay. Don't be too hard on yourself. You couldn't have known Kaden was capable of something like this. It's not your fault."

Blake's eyes snapped up. He backed away from me. "Kaden? What?"

"Yeah. Kaden." I stared at him. "Who were you thinking of?"

Ignoring my question, Blake said, "He's not—he's not even a suspect." Blake backed away even more. "What made you think he had anything to do with this?"

"You." I opened my palms toward him. "You said he might've figured out that you and Paris were together. And if he's used to protecting you, maybe he tried to stop you from making what he saw to be a terrible mistake."

"I never said any of that." He furrowed his brow as he thought back to make sure that wasn't true. "I mean, not to you."

"Zoe may have mentioned it," I muttered.

Blake stepped forward, his gaze intensifying. "Zoe was the one who told you it was my brother?"

"Well, she and I talked it through that night after we found you in the Underground. He vapes, and he had cause to want to keep Paris away from you."

"He doesn't vape." Blake shook his head definitively. "He's always on me about quitting."

"If he's around you, he had access to the liquid, which I think is how Paris died." I hoped it wouldn't get me in too much trouble that I'd just leaked the cause of death in Paris's murder.

"What about Zoe?" Blake asked.

"She doesn't vape either."

"Are you sure?" Blake watched me a little too intensely for comfort. "How well do you really know her?"

"What do you mean?" I giggled nervously. "You're the one who hired her."

"She's good at her job, but we started noticing inconsistencies. Kaden pointed it out at first, and we did a little digging."

The file they had on her.

"Yeah, the file your brother started because he found out she and I were digging into Paris's case, and he wanted to stop her." I was grasping, but only because it felt like the ground was slipping out from beneath my feet.

"Kaden didn't start the file because of that. It's because she lied to us about her name."

"Why would she do that?" I asked at the same time Zoe's comment about the police making her nervous came back to me.

Blake shot me a dark look. "Davis is a common last name, so we didn't catch it at first, but we got a hint slipped under the bar door one day asking if we knew who we'd hired. Once we did a little digging, we figured out who she was."

"And who is that?" I gulped.

"Her previous last name was Stimac," he said.

The walls of the hallway spun around me. Zoe was a Stimac? She'd just moved here from the East Coast. Could she really have come all this way just to kill Paris Elliott? Iris mentioning Zoe's surname change flashed through my mind. Thinking of Iris reminded me that she'd called earlier and left a message. I'd been so distracted with figuring out Addy's murder, then talking to Gavin, and then Laurie that I hadn't checked it yet.

I needed to know.

Holding up a finger toward Blake. I pulled my phone out of my pocket and dialed Iris's number.

"Meggie, hey." Her voice was cheerful, in total contrast to the worries whirling around in my brain. "Did you get my message?"

"Uh, I didn't listen to it yet," I croaked out. "I saw that you called, and I figured I'd just call you back." I couldn't even bring myself to ask if it was about Zoe or not. The possibility was too awful.

Iris cleared her throat. "I found out the last name Zoe and her mom went by before they changed to Davis."

I waited, sweat forming on my neck as worry pulsed through my veins. "Let me guess. It was Stimac?"

She sucked in a surprised breath. "How'd you know?"

"Lucky guess," I deadpanned.

Iris was buzzing with excitement. "I found the court order attached to the name change. Her mother, Jewel, petitioned to change it after the death of her husband."

Death? My throat felt dry.

"It's not unusual," Iris explained, taking my silence as

confusion about the process. "I mean, for the wife. If they petition, it's usually granted. But the unusual part was that she wanted to change Zoe's last name as well."

"But they approved it?" I guessed.

"They did. In the end, they agreed with Zoe's mother that the last name put her life in danger in the same way it had for her father, who'd allegedly been killed in some kind of family feud. Changing it back to Jewel's maiden name, as well as their move across the country, would ensure Zoe didn't get caught up in the feud like her father had." Iris paused. "Anyway, I've got it all printed out. I'll bring it home for your friend tonight if you'd like."

"Thanks, Iris." My words were mere whispers as I hung up.

Could Zoe really have lied to me? Had she known that the Elliotts had killed her father and come back to get revenge?

Blake watched me, eyebrows raised in a silent question. *Do you believe me now?*

My gaze flicked between him and Zoe's door across the hall. He hadn't been waiting for me at all. He was here to confront Zoe. Squeezing my eyes shut while I willed all of this to be wrong, I tried to recalibrate. "Wait. But if she's one of you, why would she try to point the finger at Kaden?"

"She's not one of us, technically," Blake spat out the statement. "Her mom never liked us, even before Sam died. Before she left, she said we'd all get what was coming to us someday, well, at least that's how my dad tells the story. I was just a baby when they left."

I swallowed. "Sam?" I thought back to Gavin telling me

one of the Stimacs had been found floating in the bay about twenty years ago. "Was that Zoe's dad?"

Blake confirmed with a nod. "Jewel and Sam had been married about five years, and their daughter was just a few months old, when he got involved in an argument with the Elliotts. They found his body in the bay a week later. Most of us aren't even sure it was the Elliotts, as easy as it usually is to blame them. But Jewel wouldn't hear of it. She blamed us and said she was going to take her daughter far away from us."

"And you think Zoe's back to ... what?" None of this felt right.

"Kaden thinks she's trying to blow up both families, teach us a lesson, make us implode completely from mutual destruction. That's how she and her mom are going to teach us one final lesson."

I couldn't believe it. Zoe was my friend. Moving to Zoe's door, I started pressing the buzzer. I needed to talk to her.

"She's not here," Blake said. "I already tried."

Right. Opal said Zoe was the one who'd let Gavin in earlier as she was leaving the building. She'd been running errands before work.

I checked my watch. "She's at work."

Blake shook his head. "She called in sick." He said it like it proved everything.

My stomach churned. This couldn't be happening. I felt it in my gut. Just as I'd been sure it couldn't have been Addy, I was sure Zoe couldn't have been involved in this.

"People saw her leaving here. She said she was on her way to run a few errands before work."

Blake coughed. "I mean, I didn't see that she wasn't at work, with my own eyes, but Kaden told me. He also said we had a light night of reservations, so I should take the day off. I came here instead."

I studied the man in front of me. He wasn't telling me the whole truth.

Tilting my head, I said, "Why would you come here instead?"

Swallowing, Blake said, "I, uh ... I was going to fire her ... for lying."

Not even qualifying his obvious lie with a verbal response, I simply crossed my arms and stared.

"Fine," he said. "I wanted to warn her that we knew and that she should turn herself in."

"The woman who you think killed the person you loved? You were going to give her a warning?" It didn't make sense. Remembering the thing he'd been fiddling with in his back pocket, I asked, "What were you going to leave her?" I snapped my fingers to show him I wasn't going to waste time being lied to anymore.

Blake closed his eyes, but he reached for his back pocket and handed over a note.

Zoe,

We know who you are and what you did to Paris. Don't come to work anymore. In fact, leave town. If not, I'm afraid Kaden is going to make sure you never do.

—Blake

When I looked up, Blake was studying me. The way his facial features were pulled taut told me he knew it didn't sound good.

"You would let her get away? You didn't want to tell the police?" I couldn't understand.

He shook his head. "Police never work out well for either of our families. It's better if they don't get involved. We've been able to handle this without the police for a hundred years."

"If you want to call what you've done *handling* it," I said with a snort. "And Kaden obviously has a temper."

Blake wouldn't meet my eyes.

My heart ached. "If Kaden told you not to come in today, but Zoe really *is* there, that might mean he's going to do something bad."

Blake didn't nod, but he didn't need to. The worry in his eyes spoke volumes.

I pulled in a shaky breath. "Okay. We need to work together, then. We don't have much time. I'll entertain the idea that Zoe could've killed Paris in retribution for her father's murder if you'll admit that Kaden might be about to harm Zoe in return."

"I can do that," Blake said, his voice hoarse.

A plan came together in my mind, and I glanced up at the roof. Knowing I was going to need ghostly backup for this, I said, "Okay. I have to grab something from my apartment, but I'll meet you down in the lobby."

Blake called the elevator while I went back into my apartment and dialed Detective Anthony's number. Biting my lip as I listened to the line ring, I willed her to still be there. But as her voicemail played, I knew she'd already headed home for the afternoon. Luckily, I also knew that she usually had her messages forwarded to her personal phone, so I hoped she would still get this.

"Hi, Detective. It's Meg Dawson from the Morrisey. I know we just spoke this morning, but there's been a recent development. That friend I was telling you about, Zoe Davis? Well, it turns out that she's actually a Stimac. I believe she thinks the Elliotts killed her father over twenty years ago, and she's a possible suspect in Paris Elliott's murder." I tried to sound sure of myself, not wanting to be wishy-washy when it came to asking the detective for help. But I couldn't just leave it at that. Groaning, I added, "To be honest, I'm not sure what I think. But I know that's what Kaden Stimac thinks, and I'm worried he might hurt her." I grabbed my purse. "I'm going to The Cooler right now with Blake Stimac. Please, please, please meet us there." I hung up.

Locking my apartment behind me, I raced up the stairwell to the roof. I didn't have time to search for the ghosts, so I hoped no one was up there as I stood at the door and called out, "Ripley! Addy!"

They appeared in front of me, Ripley's eyes slanted in a warning. "Hey, watch it. Hayden's in the greenhouse." She jerked her head to the side.

"I don't care," I panted, winded from running up the flight of stairs. Jabbing my finger into the elevator button, I added, "Zoe's in trouble. I need you to go to the speakeasy and check to see if she's there." I couldn't explain everything at that moment, but the full story could wait.

"Who are we protecting her from?" Addy asked, like a soldier waiting for orders.

"Kaden Stimac," I answered. "Blake and I will be right there."

The ghosts nodded and disappeared just as the elevator arrived, the door dinging open to let me in. I ignored the disconcerting way the whole thing dipped as I stepped inside, and then cursed the thing as it just sat there. This was one of the times when it took about seventeen seconds to get going. Added to that, the trip down felt like it took forever, but I knew it would still be faster than trying to run down all the flights to the lobby.

Blake was pacing by the wall of resident mailboxes when I arrived. He turned toward the front door, but I gestured for him to follow me in the opposite direction.

"Shortcut," I whispered, holding a finger up to my lips as I stretched up to grab the key to unlock the mechanical room. I slid it back into its hiding spot as I propped the door open and let Blake inside.

But as we made our way to the back right corner, I found the entrance to the Underground blocked. Someone had not only moved the pieces of wood back over the opening, but they'd also placed three file cabinets side by side in front of the wood, obstructing the entrance completely. A dolly sat next to them, showing that they'd recently been moved. Swearing under my breath, I guessed Detective Anthony must've called Nancy after my visit that morning and convinced her to block the staircase.

That plan foiled, I groaned, and said, "Never mind. We have to go around. Sorry."

I thought about going through the basement, but I didn't remember the combination. I couldn't very well ask Milo to help me, with Blake right there. It would just be easier to go around.

Blake and I ran out of the mechanical room and headed for the front of the Morrisey. I ignored the calls of concern coming from the Conversationalists as we sped past, pushing through the lobby doors and out onto the street. We took a left and ran around the corner toward the bar. It was locked.

We shared a worried glance as Blake pulled out a ring of keys with shaking fingers. He opened the door, and we slipped inside the dark tavern.

Twenty-Two

The bottles of liquor stacked along the back of the bar felt like an eerie audience as Blake and I crept through the Square. At least, that's what I told myself was causing the hair on the back of my neck to stand on end, making me feel as if we were being watched.

Heading through the walk-in cooler door, we jogged down the stairs into the speakeasy. It was dark, too, the only light spilling out from the partially open door to the office. Blake frowned and walked forward. I followed close behind him.

But the office was empty.

"They're not here." Blake shrugged as if that was it.

"We can't know until we check in there." I motioned to the closet that led into the Underground. "Please, Blake." I grabbed on to Blake's arm, willing him to listen.

Swallowing, Blake agreed. He put a finger to his lips as we snuck through the tunnel and into the Underground. Being this close to Blake, I caught the peachy smell of his and Paris's signature vape liquid, and I wondered if Zoe could've been the one to stick that syringe in Paris's neck.

At first, we didn't see or hear a thing, but then a man hissed, "I know it was you."

"Me, what?" Zoe responded. "I don't know what you're talking about, Kaden."

Blake and I crept forward toward a faint light in the abandoned portion of the building next door.

Zoe stood in the middle of the opening, arms crossed in a show of nonchalance. But I could see the fear in her eyes as Kaden stalked back and forth, next to her. Ripley and Addy had placed themselves in between the two, keeping Kaden in their sights as they prepared to block him if he came at her.

"Oh, Meg. You're here. Good." Addy's shoulders relaxed slightly.

At first, I worried that if the ghosts could see me, so could Kaden. But glancing down, I confirmed that Blake and I were still mostly shrouded in darkness. Addy and Ripley must've seen me purely because they'd been searching the darkness for me.

Ripley's gaze met mine. "Sorry, Megs. We wanted to tell you where we were, but we were worried that if one of us left, we wouldn't have the strength alone to stop him."

I couldn't respond but nodded in thanks.

"This guy is pretty worked up," Addy sang out in warning as Blake and I crept closer, sticking to the darkness.

Kaden let out an unhinged laugh. "You can drop the act, Zoe. Seriously, it's getting old. I know you're one of us."

"Why do you keep saying that?" Zoe let out an exasperated groan. "I don't know what you mean."

He stopped pacing and turned to face her. Addy and Ripley braced themselves.

"You're a Stimac. We found you out." He practically yelled the last part.

"What?" Zoe blinked, her arms dropping by her sides in surprise. "I'm a ... But that can't ... My mom—"

Kaden cut her off. "Your mom. Exactly. Jewel *Davis*. I barely remember her, but my parents thought she was trouble when she and Sam started dating. She tried to get Sam to move away, to leave his family behind. Even as a kid, I knew she hated us, and that only increased once Sam died."

The hurt written on Zoe's expression made me sure she hadn't known any of that. "Sam?" she whispered. "My dad ... is dead?"

"Like you didn't know." Kaden snorted.

"I promise, I didn't. Why would I move all the way across the country looking for answers about my dad?" Her voice shook with a mixture of sadness and rage.

Kaden glared at her. "So, you working for us was just a coincidence?"

"Well ... no. I knew my dad used to live at the Morrisey, and my mom mentioned The Cooler during one of her more lucid drug-induced sleep-talking sessions during her treatment. But that's it. I swear. She kept all of this from me, probably to protect me from this terrifying family, now that I think about it." Zoe's tone was dry and filled with the same hatred her mother must've felt surrounding the feud.

Shaking his head, Kaden began pacing again. "No, it had to be you. You came out to get revenge for your father's death. You killed Paris and tried to blame it on us. Your mom said we would all be sorry one day, that the feud would destroy us all. She warned us, and then she sent you when she couldn't finish it herself." The conviction behind his voice wavered as he continued to speak.

"Listen to yourself," Zoe scoffed. "That doesn't make any sense. My mom likely hated your family, but she got me as far away from you as possible. She kept the identity of my father a secret my whole life, not because she didn't want me to find *him*, but because she didn't want me to find any of *you*." Zoe shook her head. "I should've trusted her. I should never have come looking."

Relief filled me as I realized I'd been right about my new friend. Zoe really was innocent. But mixed in with those good feelings was a swirl of confusion. If Kaden had been so sure it was Zoe who killed Paris, did that mean ... he wasn't the murderer? Blake must've been equally confused because he shifted his weight, placing a hand on the wall next to us.

A loose board that had been resting there fell, clattering to the ground.

Kaden and Zoe jumped, spinning in our direction. Kaden's flashlight whirled on us, making us shield our eyes from the light.

"Blake? What are you doing here?" Kaden barked out the question.

Zoe peered into the darkness and said, "Meg?"

"I was worried about you, Zoe," I said at the same time Blake looked to his brother, pointed at me, and blurted out, "She thought you were the murderer."

I resisted rolling my eyes at how Blake immediately tossed me right under the bus, because we had bigger problems to worry about. "If it wasn't Zoe or Kaden, who killed Paris?" I exhaled the question as we all congregated together, no one circling the other, no longer predator and prey. We were equals, all without an answer to the question.

Settling on a large piece of concrete that sat in the center of the dilapidated room, I thought about Gavin. Without Kaden, Blake, or Zoe, Gavin and the guy from Boutique Liquor were my only suspects left. But Laurie's words from our terrible conversation earlier rang in my mind. "Correlation doesn't mean causation."

There was too much doubt. It didn't make sense.

"The killer had to be someone with access to the vape liquid Paris used," I said, more to myself than anything.

Blake snapped his fingers. "Her regular shipment got lost in the mail, never showed up at her apartment. She had to go in and order more in person, which she hasn't done since we started dating, just in case we were seen in the same place."

"I *thought* you two might be together," Kaden said with an exhale. The darkness of the Underground threw shadows across his face.

Blake nodded. "I was going to tell you. I just..." He glanced down at his feet.

Ripley, more focused on the vape part of Blake's earlier statement, gasped. "That's why the smoke shop was all out of that flavor. He hadn't expected Paris's double order."

"But anyone could've stolen her vape order," I said dejectedly, then frowned at Kaden. "Wait. If you weren't going to hurt Zoe, why did you bring her down here? Why not just talk in the bar?"

Zoe raised her hand. "Kaden didn't bring me in here. He

followed me. I was the one who came down here." When I squinted in question, she added, "I got a note telling me we missed a clue in the Underground, and I came to work early to look around. Well, actually, I tried going through the Morrisey first, but it was blocked off, so I came through The Cooler."

"And I was restocking the bar when I saw you come in," Kaden explained. "I thought it was weird since you'd called in sick, so I hid and followed you."

Zoe's chin jerked back. "I didn't call in sick."

Kaden snorted. "Uh, yeah ... you ... did?" His words slowed, and he tipped his head until what had started out to be so absolute ended as a question.

But I was more interested in the part about the note Zoe had gotten. "A note? From who?"

Zoe shrugged. "I sort of thought it was from you, that you'd learned something during your visit with the detective and wanted me to meet you down here. That became less likely when the Morrisey entrance was blocked, but by then I was too curious."

"So, it had to be someone who was in the building earlier today." I thought back through my day. It had been *full*, and I squeezed my eyes shut as I went through it all.

Waking up and talking to Detective Anthony.

Finding the cypher that helped us figure out the truth behind the Elliott-Stimac feud.

Addy disappearing into the Underground.

My trip below to talk to the basement ghosts.

Gavin showing up to apologize.

My call with Lau—

But my mind didn't go further. Something stuck out about the previous event. When Gavin had been in the lobby, Darius and Art had accused Opal of letting in "another one of those Elliotts." Opal had been adamant that she hadn't, that it was just their imaginations, or poor eyesight.

"It was Sophia," I whispered.

"Her sister?" Kaden scoffed. "No way."

Standing, I let the words rush out of me as soon as they came to mind. "She could've easily stolen Paris's vape liquid since they live in the same building. She's interested in chemistry and biology, so she would know that administering nicotine into the bloodstream would kill a person. I think she stole the key Blake gave Paris and used it to come through here to the Morrisey so she could access Zoe's apartment, knowing she probably wouldn't be welcome back in through the front doors of our building after the other night. Maybe the stairs were blocked by the time she came back, so she had to go out the front doors instead," I guessed.

"And she hated Paris," Blake added.

All of us turned to him.

"What?" we all asked at once.

"She and Paris never really got along," Blake said. "Paris said Sophia was always jealous of her. She was mad that Paris was the face of the company even though Sophia 'did all the work.'" He used finger quotes. "She hated that Paris got the top apartment in the building, even though Sophia wouldn't have been able to live there because it was too close to the dusty attic, and her asthma would've flared up." He snorted. "She was even mad at Paris for vaping, saying it was an affront to people with asthma everywhere that she would choose to hurt her healthy lungs."

Asthma? What if the coughing Addy heard hadn't been Paris, but Sophia? Panic coursed through me in waves, making me feel dizzy.

"Why didn't you say something sooner?" Kaden scolded his brother.

Balking at the reprimand, Blake said, "I didn't think she would *kill* her. A lot of siblings don't get along, and they don't murder each other."

He was right. "But Paris finally went too far," I said, realizing what had happened as I remembered Sophia talking to Boutique Liquor, remembered her speech during the Centennial Gin party. "Sophia said the company was going in new directions, not *big* ones."

"Paris wanted to sell the gin nationally, for it to be in every grocery store instead of working with a niche distributor like Boutique," Blake said, nodding as he understood. "She knew Sophia was going to be mad about that Boutique Liquor deal. I just didn't think she'd be *that* mad." Blake coughed.

But then I realized his coughing, my earlier dizziness, it wasn't merely from our surprise. My nostrils flared.

My voice shook as I asked, "Does anyone else smell smoke?"

Twenty-Three

Within seconds of my question, everyone was coughing and pulling their shirts up to cover their mouths as it became positive there was smoke.

Kaden ran back toward The Cooler and called out, "She put a padlock on the gate. I can't get through." Panic edged his tone, and from the thumping sound that followed, Kaden tried ramming it with his foot a few times to see if he could get it to budge.

"I'll check the alley door," Blake said before rushing over to the staircase and jogging up. "She locked the door behind her," he called down before rattling the exterior door a few times for good measure.

"Don't you guys have the keys? You own the building." Zoe's voice shook.

Kaden shook his head. "The police still have mine."

"I gave mine to Paris," Blake said. "Which I'm guessing Sophia has now."

I let my eyes slide closed as I understood. "Sophia lured us down here on purpose. And I bet she was the one who blocked off the Morrisey staircase, not the detective." That was why she'd had to risk exiting through the lobby.

"Does anyone's phone work?" Blake called out.

We all checked. Not a single one of us had service.

"So, we're stuck?" Zoe's eyes were wide, peeking up above her shirt as the smoke thickened.

My eyes stung. "No." There was one exit Sophia hadn't blocked. I sucked in a breath as I thought of the secret passage the basement ghosts had shown me earlier. I immediately regretted the gasp when I pulled in more smoke. But as soon as I remembered the safe, my stomach sank. I'd locked it behind me. There wouldn't be a way to open it again ... unless the ghosts could focus their energy enough to turn the combination.

"We have to find the fire and put it out," Kaden said. "It could hurt a lot of people if this place goes up in flames."

The Great Fire of 1889 came to mind. They'd specifically rebuilt this section of town without wood so that wouldn't happen again, but I also didn't think that was Sophia's plan.

"Sophia's not going to murder hundreds of people by setting an entire block on fire," I said aloud as I realized it. "She's a scientist. She knows we'd die of smoke inhalation long before we were burnt." I blinked as the smoke stung my eyes. "I think I can get us out of here, but I need you all to follow me."

Addy and Ripley moved ahead of me, glowing in the light of my flashlight as we moved in a line, crouching low to stay below the thin wisps of smoke.

Risking talking to the ghosts in the presence of Zoe and the Stimacs, I pretended to cough the word, "Combination," to Ripley and Addy.

Seeing where I was taking them, and understanding what they needed to do, the ghosts disappeared.

I froze as we reached the back of the safe, unsure of what to do next. Maybe I shouldn't pin all my hopes on the ghosts and the combination lock. If we all pushed on the boards at the top of the staircase, maybe we could topple those file cabinets. The group behind me called out questions about where we were going.

Picking the best option, I walked forward. "Through here," I said, motioning to the safe. "The door's stuck, so I have to push it just right," I lied, pretending to push on the door as I hoped this would work.

A moment later, Ripley returned and said, "We're trying to use our energy to do the combination. Hold on."

It wasn't like we could go anywhere. But should we work on the Morrisey exit just in case the ghosts couldn't get it? Was this really how we were going to die? The smoke hadn't seemed so bad at first, but it was definitely growing thicker. How many minutes could we last before the smoke did irreversible damage to our lungs and hearts? There was a lot of space to fill, but soon it would be hard to stay below the smoke.

Just as I was going to suggest a different plan, the safe clicked in front of me.

Crying out in relief, I pushed through into the basement of the Morrisey. I ushered Zoe, Blake, and Kaden through before closing the safe behind us to contain the smoke.

I couldn't see a single ghost in the basement as I led the group up to the stairwell. Had they all used every bit of their energy helping us? There wasn't time to think about it as we spilled into the lobby, coughing. I didn't even need to pull out my phone to call 9-1-1 because to our left, the mechanical room door was open, and firefighters were already streaming through.

Detective Anthony rushed over. "Is that all of you?" she asked.

"We're all out. It's clear." I coughed.

"Everyone's out," she called to the firefighters.

Reaching out to grab the detective's arm before she walked away, I said, "I have a feeling the fire's contained. I think she was just trying to smoke us out."

"She?" The detective cocked her hip to the side.

"Sophia Elliott killed her sister, and she tried to kill all of us," Blake said from over my shoulder.

The detective must've been getting close because understanding smoothed out her previously tight features. "Stay here. I'm going to call this in." Pulling out a radio, she stepped away from the group.

I turned to see Zoe and the Stimac brothers panting, mouths open, slightly dirty from the smoke, but smiling. Without warning, Kaden pulled Blake and then Zoe into a big hug, holding out his arm and gesturing for me to join.

"We're alive," he said with a surprised cough. "I really thought we were goners there for a minute."

Zoe puffed out her cheeks. "Me too." She turned to me. "Meg, how'd you know about that safe?"

Pressing my lips together, I said, "The Morrisey has a lot

of secrets."

A chuckle bubbled out of Blake. "I don't care how she knew. I'm just grateful it was there."

At that moment, a collection of Morrisey residents rushed over, obviously having broken through whatever barriers the police and firefighters had been enforcing. They showered me and Zoe with hugs and questions. Over the cacophony of concern, Zoe met my gaze and smiled.

Finished with my medical check, I plopped onto the lobby couch next to Zoe. I ran my shoulder into hers.

"How are your lungs?" I asked.

She coughed as if my mention of them made her remember their state. "Acceptable," she croaked. Smiling, and in a much clearer voice, she added, "No, the paramedics said I'm very lucky. We all are."

I had to agree. I wanted nothing more than to thank my ghostly pals profusely for their aid, but that would have to wait until they returned.

Ripley had only disappeared a few times. Most of those had been accidents, when she'd blasted out too much energy all at once when caught by surprise. Unlike the times when she went sketchy, disappearances like this often took days, if not weeks sometimes for her to regain her energy enough to come back in her spirit form.

The thought of being without my best friend for weeks made me feel lost, but then I remembered the woman sitting next to me, and I didn't feel so alone.

"So, you're a Stimac, huh?" I shook my head in disbelief.

"I guess so." Zoe locked eyes with me. "Hey, thanks for believing in me," she said seriously. "Blake mentioned you were the one who convinced him I was in trouble. Even though Kaden turned out to be innocent, the two of us would've been doomed down there if you hadn't been there to lead us out."

"Of course," I said. "We're basically the same person, so I knew you couldn't have been the murderer."

Zoe laughed. "We are the same. Well, except now I know who my dad was ... and that he's dead." The happiness she'd exhibited a moment ago fell away. "It's hard to feel sad about it when I never knew who he was."

"That's understandable," I said. "At least you have family to get to know."

Zoe's eyes tracked over to where Kaden and Blake were running through the same tests we'd just finished to make sure their lungs hadn't been too badly damaged by the smoke. And even though neither of them turned out to be a killer, there was a hesitation to Zoe's nod.

"The Stimacs will be ... interesting to get to know better," she said carefully. "But I'm wary of getting too involved with them after everything. Well, that and knowing that my mom specifically kept me away from the family. It feels a little like I'm not honoring her wishes if I allow them into my life."

"I think it's a decision you'll have to make for yourself," I countered. "Your mom made the one she thought was best at the time, but this new generation of Stimacs has more motivation to finally lay this feud to rest. Maybe you can help them do that."

"I can definitely try, if they'll take my help." Zoe cast a quick glance in my direction. "But I'm not worried so much about my Stimac family because I feel like I already have such a great start with the Morrisey residents. The way they surrounded me back there, and you sticking up for me..." A tear cascaded down Zoe's cheek.

"They're a pretty great family," I said as warmth spread through my body.

She turned to me. "You don't feel like I'm coming in and trying to take that from you, do you? Because if you did, I would—"

I held up a hand to stop her from getting any further with that statement. "Not at all. My Morrisey family is your Morrisey family. Believe me, they have *more* than enough love and attention to go around." I indicated to where Nancy was talking to one of the paramedics, taking notes about our care and what signs to look for if our conditions worsened.

Zoe leaned her head against mine.

It wasn't long before the detective came over to take our statements. We had to do that separately, but once we were back together, Detective Anthony let us know that they'd caught Sophia and charged her with the murder of her sister, as well as the attempted murder of the four of us.

"She confessed right there," the detective shared. "It didn't hurt that her purse reeked of the same peach-flavored vape liquid she used to kill her sister. Apparently, she spilled a bunch when she was trying to fill the syringe, and then again when she jumped Paris." Detective Anthony arched an eyebrow at me. "That's why Paris's body smelled so strongly of the stuff."

And why I'd smelled peaches when Zoe and I had been at Emmie's that day for lunch. It had been her purse, not peach pie, as Zoe had first thought.

"She'd hoped to plant even more evidence at the scene to point to Blake, knowing he was supposed to meet Paris there that evening. She was going to call in an anonymous tip, hoping that we'd catch him at the scene and he'd be arrested, but she heard you and panicked, leaving in a hurry."

"But once Blake turned out to have an alibi, she started to look into pinning it on someone else ... Zoe," I said. "That's why she'd researched you," I told my friend. "How she knew that you worked for the Stimacs. And, probably what your real last name was."

"She was also likely the person who kept slipping them notes about me," Zoe scoffed.

Detective Anthony nodded resolutely. "Well, Sophia won't be bothering you anymore." The woman added a rare grin at the end of the statement.

"Thank you, Detective," I said, hoping my tone held all the sincerity I felt. "I'm sorry I keep relying on your workaholic tendencies." I held up a hand. "I promise you won't see the likes of me or the Morrisey in the near future, if I can help it."

She let out a dry laugh. "Oh, Meg. Let's not make

promises you can't keep." She smirked and then walked away.

Zoe lifted her chin. "I like her."

I did too. And she'd called me Meg. I counted that as a major win. You know, on top of being alive.

Twenty-Four

By the time they released Zoe and me, and we had assured all of our concerned Morrisey neighbors we were okay, the sun was just dipping below the horizon.

It had been a long day, and part of me wanted nothing more than to collapse onto my bed for twelve hours straight. But the other, bigger part of me felt weird sitting in my apartment alone. Anise was there, of course, and I grinned at her crazy kitten zoomies while I fixed myself something to eat. But Ripley and Addy's absence left a hole that I didn't think a familiar movie or even the right soundtrack would help fill tonight.

Counting—on my fingers because I was still not that great at the math—I found it was just about lunchtime in Japan. I wet my lips, swiped a wet paper towel over my face to get the worst of the smoke that had gathered there, and called Laurie.

I didn't know if he would even answer. He'd been the

one who'd gotten upset during our last call, after all. Should I have given him space and waited until he called me? I didn't know the etiquette. All I knew was that I was sorry I'd doubted his friend, and I wanted to hear his voice more than anything at that moment.

The best sound in the world rang out as Laurie accepted my call. He appeared on my screen.

"Hey, I'm so glad you called." Laurie ran a hand down his face. "I've felt awful all day, and I was going to call you to apologize—"

"What do you have to apologize for?" I asked. "I'm the one who accused your friend of murder."

Laurie's eyes went wide. "I talked to Gavin."

My breath caught. Oh no. Had Laurie told him I'd suspected him?

He must've caught the worry in my expression, because he said, "Don't worry. I didn't say anything about the case. I made him tell me about the ball in more detail. I didn't realize he'd treated you like that, Meg. I'm so sorry." Something like fear passed behind his eyes.

"What?" I asked.

Laurie swallowed. "Well, it's just ... after he told me, he mentioned he was going to talk to Foster Elliott about the galleries to make it all up to you. I didn't know he had so much pull with the Elliotts. There's a lot about him I don't know. Like, I don't know for sure that he isn't guilty. I should have listened to you."

There was such obvious panic coursing through Laurie at the thought that his friend might be involved in the murder that I had to put a swift end to that feeling.

"Don't worry," I blurted. "I know *for sure* that he isn't."

Tilting his head, Laurie studied me. "Why? What happened?"

"It's a long story, and I think you might be on a lunch break or still at work?" Even when I did the math, I never trusted that I'd gotten the answer correct.

Laurie laughed. "I would be just getting back from lunch, but I took the rest of the day off after my meeting finished, so we're good."

"Not because of our fight, I hope," I said.

He chewed on his lips. "I mean, sort of. I snapped at you, and it surprised me, honestly. After we hung up, I thought about how stressed I've been and how I haven't really had a moment to breathe since I got here." He massaged the back of his neck. "The times when I've been the happiest are when I've been able to text with you or see your face."

"I'm glad you've gotten some time off today, then." I noticed he was in a T-shirt instead of the fancy suit he'd been wearing earlier. "Though I don't think it was fair of me to call you before work and dump all of that on you." I winked. "So, go easy on yourself."

He nodded in concession.

"What did you do with your time off?" I asked, settling back into the couch and resting my head on the armrest.

Laurie beamed. "I took a train to a rather large Buddha statue. And I ate some amazing food. It really is pretty here. You'd want to paint everything."

"I probably would." I chuckled. "You'll have to send me some pictures."

He nodded, but the motion jerked to a stop as he

narrowed his eyes. "Wait, weren't you going to tell me a long story about how you know Gavin isn't Paris's killer?"

"Oh!" My eyes went wide. "I almost forgot."

That's what Laurie did to me. He made everything else fade into the background in the best way possible.

"Yes, but only if you're sitting down," I said, prepping him. "It's wild and rather long."

"Wild and long are my favorite kinds of stories." Laurie gave me a sexy smile.

Twenty-Five

Seven days later ...

IT WAS ANOTHER SCORCHER, and I was really starting to wonder if I should get an AC unit for my apartment as sweat dripped down my temple. Then again, I was wrestling large canvases into a bag, so maybe my sweat had more to do with the activity than the heat.

I'd just zipped the last paintings into the huge tote bag when I heard a familiar voice call out a greeting.

"Honey, I'm home." Ripley whooshed into the room, wearing a face-splitting grin.

I swiped a hand across my sweaty forehead. "Yay! I'm so glad you're here."

"What's going on?" Ripley tapped her foot as she took in the packed portfolio. "Did you get a gallery job? Are they going to hang your art?" Glancing around the room, she asked, "How long have I been gone?"

Laughing at the barrage of questions, I said, "You've been gone a week, and yes, I got a couple of offers from the galleries who'd previously said no."

Whether it had been Gavin's urging, or Foster Elliott's guilt surrounding his daughter trying to kill me, I didn't know. However, a few days after Sophia was arrested, I got an email from one gallery, letting me know they'd reconsidered and would love to interview me for a position. The funky gallery in Pioneer Square had called, too, letting me know they had an opening, after all.

"Which one did you go with?" Ripley asked, eyes shining with excitement.

"Neither." When she blinked in confusion, I said, "I decided I'm not going to work at a gallery."

Ripley frowned, fatigue playing at the edges of her expression. She'd just gotten me out of the mindset that I needed to quit art, and I could see that she didn't want to go through that again.

I laughed. "Not because I'm quitting. But I found a better option. Zoe saw my Addy painting, and she loved it. She's been trying to get the guys to update the décor in The Cooler, but nothing seemed to go with the historic pictures, and they were resistant to let those go. Well, she took one of the paintings to them to see what they thought, and it sold before she could even show it to them."

Ripley sucked in an excited breath. Then her eyes flicked to the place where Addy's painting still hung on my wall.

"Don't worry, it was the blonde. I told her that one's not

for sale. I'm keeping it." I patted the portfolio at my side. "But Blake and Kaden asked for more right away, saying if I let them hang them in The Cooler, I could put prices on them for people to buy."

"Like a coffee shop?" Ripley squinted.

"Yeah, but hopefully even better. The people who drink and eat at The Cooler are usually dropping quite a bit of money, so I'm hoping they'll be open to spending some on art too. I've spent the last week tweaking those twenties' girls with the cats I started, adding to the collection, and framing them. Turns out that without you around, I don't know what to do with myself, so I did a lot of painting." I chuckled.

Ripley folded her arms in front of her. "And talking to Laurie, I hope."

I nodded. "Lots of that."

"You two made up?"

"We did."

Other than Zoe, Laurie had been my biggest cheerleader when it came to selling my art at The Cooler. He'd even helped me come up with a logo that I loved and had designed cards with the title of each piece, along with the price. I'd printed them out and had them all ready for the Stimacs to hang next to each painting. He was going to help me with a website as soon as his workload slowed.

"Can I see?" Ripley asked, eyes bright. "Or do I have to wait until they're hanging downstairs?"

I wrinkled my nose. "It was really hard to get them in that bag..."

Before Ripley could give me a hard time, another voice trilled out a greeting.

"Ladies!" Addy's familiar voice felt like a ray of sunshine as she rushed into the apartment. "Omigosh, I'm so glad you're okay, Meg." Addy covered her mouth with her hands. "I was so worried there at the end with all that smoke, and then we were trying our hardest with that combination." She turned to Ripley, who looked cool as a cucumber. "Have you been back a lot longer than me? Did you already go over all of this?"

Ripley and I shared an amused look.

"We haven't," I said with a chuckle.

"I just got back too," Ripley told her. "I knew once we unlocked the safe, Meg would get them out of there. She's a fighter."

"Yes. Everyone is healthy," I assured them. "Sophia is awaiting her trial, but rumor has it that she's going to plead guilty." My eyes widened. "Oh, and Addy, you'll be happy to hear that the Stimacs and Elliotts have officially called a truce in their feud."

Addy jumped up and down. "What? How?" The movement made her dress swish and Ani raced over from where she'd been hanging out on the windowsill to swat at her.

Refocusing on Addy's question about the truce, I buffed my fingernails on my tank top strap and said, "I may have sent both families an anonymous letter with the recipe cypher picture and some 'authentic' diary entries from one Addison Elliott explaining the situation, found stuffed in the handbag next to her bones a century too late."

Detective Anthony might not have enough hard evidence

yet to officially assign an identity to Addy's skeleton, but the feuding families didn't need to know that. All they needed to know was that it was all a misunderstanding.

"You faked diary entries from me?" Addy placed a hand on her chest as if she were upset, but the wide smile that followed told me she approved.

"Don't worry, I added a few of your stories about parties and boys for posterity. Milo and the guys helped me get the lingo and the details right," I assured her. When she and Ripley sent me questioning glances, I said, "The basement guys showed up a few days before you two." I shrugged, not sure why there had been the discrepancy between the spirits.

Addy and Ripley looked at one another and nodded. They knew.

"We did the last push together. Milo had just finished the last turn on the combination when he disappeared," Ripley explained. "But Addy and I knew you still needed the lever unlocked to open it. We put everything we had behind that push."

"I'm so glad it worked." Addy smiled as she looked around the apartment. "And it sounds like my business surrounding the feud is officially finished." Even as she said it, her spirit dimmed. A ray of light passed through her as she walked by the window, and it glinted off her spirit in the most brilliant way. Ani galloped over, claws splayed as she chased the beads, unaware of what was happening.

My eyes filled with tears. They were happy tears, mostly, but it was still hard to say goodbye.

"You could stick around for a bit, just to make sure they

don't mess things up again," Ripley said. Even my sarcastic, grunge-loving best friend teared up at the prospect.

Addy turned to us. But instead of her eyes being filled with tears, they were wide with hope. "I'm excited to see what's next, actually. It feels like I'm waiting to get into a really swell party."

I swiped at the tears streaming down my face. "Have fun, Addy."

"We'll miss you," Ripley said.

And then, our flapper friend was gone.

Ripley took a moment to compose herself before she looked at me. "Well, kid. Looks like it's just me and you again."

My lips tugged into a grin, and I dried my eyes. "I wouldn't have it any other way." But worry engulfed me as I watched my best friend. For the first time in a while, I couldn't read the enigmatic expression on her face. "Are you okay?" I nodded toward the place Addy had just been standing. "I mean, you just lost Clark, and now Addy."

The way Ripley had begged Addy to stay made my heart ache.

But instead of crying or moping like she had with Clark, Ripley straightened her shoulders. "You know what? I think I'm okay. There's still a lot for me to do around here."

I arched an eyebrow in her direction.

Ripley laughed. "*Not* mothering you. I learned my lesson. I know you don't need that anymore. But I hope you still have room in your life for a friend." She looked down before carefully meeting my gaze.

The hesitation I saw instead of her usual confidence

made everything feel wobbly. I didn't falter before nodding, and then I added, "Only a best friend, though."

Ripley's mouth tugged into a smile, but it faded as she grew contemplative. "I thought a lot while I was sketched out," she said. "I've always had a defeatist outlook on my unfinished business, but I also haven't ever really tried to figure it out."

"Because of me." I swallowed the lump that clogged my throat at that admission.

Ripley shrugged. "Maybe, but now that you're older, and you don't need looking after twenty-four seven"—she winked at me to show me she was mostly joking—"maybe I should figure out why I'm really here."

Sadness swirled through me, but it wasn't as biting and hurtful as it used to be when I thought of Ripley someday moving on. This most recent depression had been rough on her, and if she was ready to move on, I wanted her to be happy.

Holding her gaze with mine, I said, "Well, I'm here to help, whatever you need."

The smile that Ripley adopted at my words made all the sadness feel worth it.

"You *are* getting pretty good at solving mysteries," she said, jabbing an elbow toward me.

I laughed. "As long as your unfinished business doesn't include me stumbling on more dead bodies, I'm in."

And even though Ripley hadn't been there when the detective made a similar joke last week, she winked and said, "Oh, Meg. You know I don't make promises I can't keep."

The Morrisey will return ...

A Poisoned Package

After two murders on the premises, the manager of the Morrisey has cracked down on who has access to the building, buying the residents a few months of peace. But the increased security hasn't made them immune to porch pirates. Packages are disappearing almost as soon as they're delivered.

The joke is on the thief when one of the packages contains poisoned truffles, and they consume what was meant for someone else. Another body in the Morrisey puts a damper on the upcoming holiday season.

Learning she was the intended target of the chocolates, overly dramatic Winnie Wisteria is inconsolable and quick to point fingers. But as the threats escalate, secretive Winnie must let the other residents into her life if she wants to stay alive. Helping her figure out who wants her dead takes Meg and her ghostly pals into the spotlight of Seattle's theater scene. But when everyone's acting, who can Meg believe? And will she find the killer before it becomes someone's final curtain call?

Get your copy today!

Join Eryn Scott's mailing list to learn about new releases and sales!

ALSO BY ERYN SCOTT

STONEYBROOK MYSTERIES

Ongoing series * Farmers market * Recipes * Crime solving twins * Cats!

A MURDER AT THE MORRISEY MYSTERY SERIES

Ongoing series * Friendly ghosts * Quirky downtown Seattle building

Pebble Cove Teahouse Mysteries

Completed series * Friendly ghosts * Oregon Coast * Cat mayors

Whiskers and Words Mysteries

Ongoing series * Best friends * Bookshop full of cats

PEPPER BROOKS COZY MYSTERY SERIES

Completed series * Literary mysteries * Sweet romance * Cute dog

About the Author

Eryn Scott lives in the Pacific Northwest with her husband and their quirky animals. She loves classic literature, musicals, knitting, and hiking. She writes cozy mysteries and women's fiction.

Join her mailing list to learn about new releases and sales!

www.erynscott.com